Left Holding the Bag

a quilting cozy

Carol Dean Jones

Publisher: Amy Marson

Creative Director: Gailen Runge

Acquisitions Editor: Roxane Cerda

Managing Editor: Liz Aneloski

Project Writer: Teresa Stroin

Technical Editor / Illustrator: Linda Johnson

Cover/Book Designer: April Mostek

Production Coordinator: Tim Manibusan

Production Editor: Alice Mace Nakanishi

Photo Assistant: Mai Yong Vang

Cover photography by Lucy Glover of C&T Publishing, Inc.

Cover quilt: *Left Holding the Bag*, 2016, by the author

Published by C&T Publishing, Inc., P.O. Box 1456, Lafayette, CA 94549

Library of Congress Cataloging-in-Publication Data

Names: Jones, Carol Dean, author.

Title: Left holding the bag : a quilting cozy / Carol Dean Jones.

Description: Lafayette, California : C&T Publishing, [2018] | Series: Quilting cozy series ; book 10

Identifiers: LCCN 2018003614 | ISBN 9781617457340 (softcover)

Subjects: LCSH: Quilting--Fiction. | Retirees--Fiction. | Retirement communities--Fiction. | GSAFD: Mystery fiction.

Classification: LCC PS3610.O6224 L44 2018 | DDC 813/.6--dc23

LC record available at https://lccn.loc.gov/2018003614

Printed in the USA

10 9 8 7 6 5 4 3 2 1

A Quilting Cozy Series

by Carol Dean Jones

Acknowledgments

I want to express my sincere appreciation to four very special friends: Janice Packard, Joyce Frazier, Sharon Rose, and Phyllis Inscoe, all of whom have spent many hours reading these chapters, bringing plot inconsistencies and errors to my attention, and providing me with their endless encouragement and support.

Thank you, dear friends, for all your hard work and for bringing fun and friendship to what could otherwise have been a tedious endeavor.

I also want to thank my readers. Many of you have stayed with me for the long haul, following Sarah and her cohorts from the beginning.

Chapter 1

"Some woman is moving into your house," Sophie announced excitedly when Sarah answered the phone.

"My house? What do you mean?"

"Your old house," Sophie explained. "There's a van out there, and I saw them carry in two sewing machines. Do you suppose she quilts?" Sophie added eagerly.

When Sarah first moved to the retirement community, she lived in a one-story townhome directly across the street from Sophie. Since that time, Sarah had married a retired detective and moved to a single-family home just a few blocks away and still within the community.

"She may be a quilter," Sarah responded. "I'm sure we'll find out soon. Let's give her time to get settled, and then perhaps we can stop by and welcome her."

"Great idea, and that's why I'm calling," Sophie responded. "I just made an apple pie, and I'm taking it over. Do you want to come with me?"

"Aren't the movers still there?" Sarah asked.

"Yes, but …"

"Sophie, slow down. Let the poor woman get moved in before descending on her." Sophie was always eager to get involved when new people moved into Cunningham Village and had been a godsend to Sarah when she arrived, alone and feeling desolate. After her husband had died and her daughter had convinced her to move into a retirement community, she had lost everything that was familiar to her. And that's when Sophie came knocking on her door. Remembering how much that visit had meant to her, Sarah began to back down. "Maybe we could just stop by for a minute and welcome her," she said hesitantly.

"That's exactly what I was thinking. Come on over, and we'll take the pie to her. And bring ice cream if you have any."

Sarah sighed and pulled a container of French vanilla ice cream from the freezer still holding the phone. She was glad to be getting rid of it since it had been a constant struggle to keep Charles on the diet his doctor had ordered after his most recent stroke.

"I'm on my way," Sarah replied, hanging up the phone and reaching for a jacket. It was mid-April, and there was a nip in the air earlier when she let Barney out.

Sarah felt somewhat better about descending upon the new neighbor once she turned the corner and saw that the moving van was pulling away. *At least she's alone now*, Sarah assured herself. *It won't seem quite so intrusive.*

Sophie was waiting on her porch when Sarah walked up with Barney in tow. "Your dog's coming with us?" Sophie commented in a disapproving tone.

"No, I thought Barney could stay in your backyard and play with Emma until we get back."

"Good idea," Sophie exclaimed. "Emma's been moping around here all morning waiting for Norman." Sophie's new gentleman friend had been dropping by most mornings for coffee and had been taking Emma to the dog park. "My hip's been acting up, and I haven't been walking her much. We just wait for Norman, but I haven't heard from him this morning," she added looking disappointed. "Maybe he's not coming today."

Sarah smiled to herself, thinking how good Norman has been for her friend. They got together almost daily and sent text messages back and forth when they were apart.

"Oh, there he is now," Sophie exclaimed, looking down at her phone which had just signaled an incoming text. "Oh," she said reading his message. "He's not coming until later, but he wants to take me to lunch. Wait a minute while I respond." She sat down and punched a few buttons, then slipped the phone back into her pocket and smiled impishly. "He'll be here in an hour."

When Sarah tapped on the door that used to be her own, it was opened by a tall, attractive woman who appeared to be somewhat younger than most of the village residents. "I'd say she's in her early sixties," Sarah was to tell her husband Charles later.

Sarah and Sophie introduced themselves, and Sophie handed the woman the tote bag which contained the pie and ice cream. She pointed out that the pie was hot and the ice cream cold and that the woman might want to separate them right away. Sarah knew Sophie was hoping for a serving of each, but their new neighbor took them into the kitchen and stuck them both in the refrigerator. Sophie started to suggest that she leave the pie out since it was warm, but Sarah poked her and shook her head.

"I'm Bernice Jenkins," the woman said, "and you'll have to excuse the mess …"

"We know what it's like to be moving," Sarah responded, hoping to put the woman at ease. "Is there anything we can do to help?" Sarah glanced around the room, looking for something familiar, but with the boxes and drop clothes, she didn't see anything of her old home.

Sophie was still waiting for an invitation to sit and have pie and ice cream, but the invitation never came. "I appreciate the thought. That was very kind of you both," the woman said as she walked back toward the front door. "I hope we can get together soon and get to know each other, but right now I've got to start dealing with these boxes. Again, thank you." By that time, she had the front door open, and there was no choice but for Sarah and Sophie to walk through it and cross the street to Sophie's house.

"That was strange," Sophie said once they were inside. Sarah went into Sophie's kitchen to let the dogs in and returned to the living room where Sophie was now sitting by the window.

"It was indeed strange," Sarah agreed, "but she just arrived and probably is overwhelmed by all the work ahead of her."

"I suppose you're right," Sophie responded, "but it felt like a major brush-off to me."

A few minutes later they heard a car pull up. Sophie peeked through the curtains and announced that a straggly looking young man was getting out of the car. "Now the car's pulling away and the guy just walked into Bernice's house without knocking."

"I'm sure it's okay, Sophie. Let's make a pot of tea."

"I don't know," Sophie replied shaking her head. "That rusted-out heap of a car and that ragtag guy—something just doesn't seem right."

Nothing else was said about the new neighbor until Sophie and Sarah sat down to tea. "I just hope that guy isn't over there eating my apple pie," Sophie grumbled.

* * * * *

"How old was the guy?" Charles asked after Sarah caught him up on her morning activities with Sophie.

"I didn't see him, but Sophie said he looked like he might be in his early twenties, but she said it was hard to tell. She said he looked unkempt, like some of the homeless men that come to the soup kitchen where she volunteers. But Bernice must have known him. He walked right in without knocking."

"She might have been expecting him, and that's why you and Sophie got the brush-off when you took Sophie's pie and my ice cream to her."

"First of all, it wasn't your ice cream. I bought that for the kids when they're here. Your lowfat, sugar-free ice cream is right there in the freezer, but you might be right about what felt like a brush-off. He arrived shortly after we left."

"How long did he stay?"

"We didn't see him leave, but we were in the kitchen. He might still be there for all I know."

At that moment, the phone rang.

"Hi, Sophie," Sarah answered. "I thought you were going out to lunch?"

"Norman and I just left, but I noticed that Bernice's car is gone now."

"She's probably gone to the store," Sarah responded.

"I could see her in the kitchen. She doesn't have her curtains up yet."

"And you think maybe the man that was there took her car?"

"I believe that's possible."

Sarah had the phone on speaker so she could continue stirring the stew she was warming up for lunch, and the conversation caught Charles' attention. "What difference does it make where the car is?" Charles asked. "Maybe the guy is family and he borrowed her car, or maybe he went shopping for her."

"I don't know," Sophie responded, hearing Charles' comment. "He didn't look like any family I'd want to have."

"My unsolicited advice," Charles began, "would be for you women to pull in your antennae and get out of this newcomer's business."

"My feeling exactly," a male voice on Sophie's end announced emphatically. Apparently, Sophie was using the speaker as well.

"Hi, Norman," Charles called. "Thanks for the support."

"You bet," Norman responded. "Do you two want to go into Hamilton with us tonight? A client gave me four tickets to the stage play *Moon Over the Mountain*."

Charles and Sarah looked at one another and shrugged. "Might as well," Sarah mouthed to her husband.

"We're in," Charles responded.

"We'll pick you up at 7:00," Norman replied.

Sophie had met Norman Hill the previous summer when he was making a presentation at the Cunningham Village community center. Norman was a semi-retired event planner. He owned Top of the Hill, a very successful event-planning company specializing in weddings and had attempted to retire more than once, but was always drawn back in by his love of the business.

"That will be fun," Sarah commented as she hung up. Turning to Charles, she asked, "What are your plans for the afternoon?"

"I'm going to the gym for a while and then a steam," he responded looking pleased with himself as he added, "Just as the doctor ordered."

"I think I'll come along," Sarah replied. She didn't want to work out at the gym other than spending some time on the treadmill, but the idea of lounging in the Jacuzzi after a rigorous swim in the indoor pool appealed to her.

At precisely 7:00, a Mercedes pulled up in front of the Parker's house, and Norman hopped out to open the doors for Sarah and Charles.

"Bernice's car is still missing," Sophie said once her friends were settled in the back seat.

"Charles has convinced me to mind my own business," Sarah responded with a wink.

"Okay. Come over in the morning, and we'll mind our own business together."

"It's a deal."

Norman caught Charles' eye in the rearview mirror and shook his head.

"What can you do?" Charles replied with a hopeless shrug.

Chapter 2

When Sarah arrived at Sophie's house the next morning, Bernice's front door was open, and Bernice was walking toward the curb with a trash bag in one hand and several boxes in the other. Sarah waved and Bernice nodded. She continued toward the curb and added her items to the pile. She gave Sarah a quick wave once her hands were free and returned to her house, closing the door behind her.

Not a very talkative person, Sarah thought as she continued toward Sophie's door.

"I see you tried to engage our new neighbor," Sophie said as she opened the door for Sarah.

"She's probably just involved in getting settled."

"She's been carrying boxes out to the curb all morning," Sophie responded, confirming Sarah's suspicion that her friend was spending her time behind the curtain at the front window.

"Did the car ever get returned? I see it's not there again this morning."

"No, he never brought it back."

"What do you think is going on?"

"I have no idea," Sophie responded, "but let's talk about it in the kitchen. I just baked cinnamon buns for us to have with our coffee."

"You're determined to fatten me up, aren't you?"

"I can't be the only chubby one," Sophie announced. "Eat up," she added as she placed the platter of steaming buns on the table and began pouring coffee. Barney gently tugged on Sarah's pant leg, and she realized Emma was in the backyard and Barney was eager to join her.

They had just settled down and were enjoying their snack when there was a tapping at the front door. "I wonder who that is?" Sophie said as she carefully stood and waited a moment before moving until her knees and hips were adequately engaged. "This getting old is for the birds," she muttered as she finally headed for the door.

"It might be Charles," Sarah called after her. "I forgot my cell phone, and he might be bringing it to me. He keeps telling me he wants me to have it with me at all times."

"Not a bad idea," Sophie responded. "Norman says the same thing." Sarah smiled to herself, knowing that until Sophie met her new gentleman friend, she had refused to even own a cell phone. Now she carried one in her pocket so she wouldn't miss his calls.

When Sophie opened the door, she was taken aback to find Bernice Jenkins standing there. Recovering quickly, Sophie greeted her enthusiastically and invited her to join them in the kitchen.

"I hope you don't mind me stopping in like this," Bernice began apologetically, "but I saw that your friend was here, and I just had to apologize to both of you for my behavior yesterday."

"No need for that," Sophie responded. "Come on in." Sophie led her guest back to the kitchen saying jovially, "We're pigging out on cinnamon buns, and we need your help with it. Sarah, look who's here!"

"Bernice," Sarah greeted her with a warm smile, hiding her surprise. "I'm glad you came by. My friend and I were just talking about something we wanted to ask you."

"I hope I can answer your question," she responded, "but first, I want to apologize to you both. I know I rushed you ladies out yesterday. I was embarrassed about the state of my house and totally overwhelmed by all those boxes. I can't imagine how my few belongings can fill so many boxes!"

Sarah and Sophie both chuckled and nodded their agreement. "But it will all disappear once you get things put into the closets and cupboards," Sarah assured her. "I just went through it not that long ago."

"You just moved here?" Bernice responded looking surprised.

"No, I've been here four years now, but I moved into a single-family home."

"Here in the Village?"

"Yes," Sarah responded.

"In fact," Sophie interjected, "she moved out of the town-home you're moving into."

"Really?" Bernice responded, looking surprised. "Why did you move?"

Sophie, not giving Sarah a chance to respond, said, "Sarah met this very handsome gentleman, fell in love, married him, and together they moved into their own home just a few blocks away on Sycamore Court."

"That's nice," Bernice responded warmly, smiling at Sarah. "So there's life after sixty, I guess?"

"There sure is, especially here in Cunningham Village," Sophie responded. "Just wait until I take you over to the community center. You won't believe your eyes. Have a seat, and I'll pour you a cup of coffee," she added gesturing to the empty chair as she reached into the cupboard for a mug.

There was a scratching at the back door and Sophie opened it, letting the dogs in. "I hope you don't mind dogs," she said addressing Bernice.

"I love animals," she answered. "I was thinking about getting a cat, but …" She didn't finish the sentence because she was now surrounded by two excited dogs competing for her attention.

"Okay," Sophie began once she got the dogs settled down. "On to what we want to ask you. First of all, I'll have to admit to being that nosey neighbor who watches moving vans being unloaded to see what the new neighbors own, and we want to ask you about those sewing machines I saw going in. You sew?"

"I don't make clothes or anything if that's what you mean. I only use my machine for quilting."

"You quilt!" Sarah exclaimed. "That's what we were hoping. I've been quilting for a few years, and Sophie here is just starting, and she's quilting by hand. She made her first quilt for her son and my daughter who just got married."

"To each other?" Bernice asked, looking surprised.

"Yes, to each other," Sarah responded proudly. "My daughter, Martha, met Sophie's son, Timothy, when he was here visiting from Alaska where he was working on the pipeline."

"He retired this past year," Sophie interjected, "and moved here with his teenage daughter, Penny. He and Martha got married this past summer."

"They're a family already," Bernice exclaimed. "That sounds really nice, especially for you two."

Sophie and Sarah looked at each other and Bernice could immediately see how close these two friends were. "We are both thrilled about it, and I have a granddaughter now!" Sophie responded as she stood up to get the coffee pot. As she was refilling their cups, she said, "So, how long have you been quilting, Bernice?"

"Well, I got started not long after my mother died," she began.

"Sorry," Sarah said.

"It was a long time ago," Bernice said responding to Sarah's sympathetic tone. "My mother left two sewing machines and a room filled with fabric and projects she had started. I just couldn't let it go, so I took a class and started making charity quilts for Children's Services."

"Children's Services?" Sarah asked.

"They investigate reports of abuse and neglect and sometimes have to remove children from their homes. They like to have quilts on hand for these children."

"That's an excellent idea," Sarah responded. "Quilts can be very comforting to children."

"The police also keep a few in the trunk of their cruisers for emergencies," Bernice added.

"How did you get started with this?" Sarah asked. She had been making charity quilts with her quilt club, but primarily they made lap quilts for people in the homeless shelters and for the elderly in nursing homes. They'd been searching for new projects.

"My husband and I never had children, and we became foster parents back in the 1980s."

"That's wonderful," Sarah responded, "but it must have been difficult."

"The hardest part was saying goodbye. Those poor kids often got returned to their parents where they'd been abused and neglected in the past. I rarely got to know how they turned out," she added.

"Is your husband with you?" Sophie asked as delicately as she could. She hadn't seen an older man during the move.

"No, Harold died a few years back," she responded sadly. The three women sat quietly, each lost in her own thoughts. *Life can turn on a dime*, Sarah thought, her mind turning to her own husband and his health problems.

Suddenly, Sophie announced, "How did this party become so maudlin?" She reached for another cinnamon bun and added, "Tell us about all that fabric your mother left."

Bernice cheered up as she talked about her mother's stash of fabric. "She had lots of different kinds of fabric, but I was only interested in the cottons. I took the rest over to the senior center. But there were also these trunks in the barn full of old fabric that I was going to just toss out, when the man who was appraising the furniture got all excited about what he called, the 'boxes of vintage yard goods.'"

"Vintage yard goods?" Sophie repeated. "What does that mean?"

"I didn't know, but I took an armload of it to this quilt shop in her hometown to see what I could find out. There were scraps of silk and velvet that I recognized from mother's crazy quilts, but what the shopkeeper got excited about was what she called 'the feedsacks.'"

"Feedsacks?" Sophie repeated. "You mean those bags the chicken feed came in when I was a girl?"

"Exactly."

"And that was exciting?" Sophie responded curiously. "Did women use them for sewing?"

"They sure did. They made clothes and quilts with them back in the early 1900s," Beatrice responded. "It was hard for women to get their hands on new fabric in those days."

"I never heard of any of this," Sarah responded. "Do people still use it?"

"The woman at the shop told me that companies stopped printing the bags when reasonably priced printed cotton became abundant, but it was still being used in the early 1950s. When mother died, she had three steamer trunks packed solid with feedsacks stored in the old barn."

"And you kept them?"

"I did. I had a basement, so it wasn't a problem, but when I moved here, I didn't know what to do with them."

"You brought them?" Sarah asked excitedly.

"I sure did, and I have no idea what to do with them now. I can't store all those trunks."

"I'd love to see the feedsacks someday, once you get settled," Sarah said. "It sounds interesting."

The women continued to chat about quilting and devoured most of the cinnamon buns. Sophie wanted to ask about Bernice's straggly visitor the previous day but decided that would be intrusive. Besides, she'd already admitted to spying on her once and was reluctant to admit to it a second time. She did wonder, though, about the car and decided she could ask that one question innocuously.

"I noticed that your car has been gone for a couple of days. Do you need a ride to the store?"

Bernice seemed to freeze for a moment but responded, "No, but thank you. A friend borrowed it, but he'll probably be bringing it back today. In fact, I expected him last night, but …" She quickly changed the subject, looking away as she stood. "I've got to get back to my boxes, but thank you so much for this pleasant break."

Something is wrong, Sarah told herself. She noticed that the woman was no longer making eye contact with either of them. *Something is definitely wrong.*

Before reaching the front door, Bernice turned to them and said, "Why don't you two come by in the morning, and I'll show you the feedsacks. I should have enough boxes out of the way by then."

"I'm going to be away for a couple of days," Sophie responded, "but Sarah, you go ahead and go. I can see them later on."

Sarah looked at Sophie inquisitively but could tell Sophie didn't want to explain at that moment. Turning to Bernice, Sarah replied, "I'd love to come if you're sure it's not an imposition. I know you have lots to do."

"I get up early, and I'll be looking forward to a break," Bernice responded. "Come around 10:00, and we'll have coffee."

As soon as Sophie closed the front door, Sarah bombarded her with questions. "Away? You'll be away? And just where are you going, and why don't I know about it?"

"We've planned a little getaway," Sophie responded mysteriously, "and I'm not sure I'm ready to talk about it."

"You may not be ready to talk about it, my friend, but it just so happens I'm ready to hear about it. Talk!"

"Okay, so Norman and I are driving down to Kentucky this weekend. He wants to look at a few cabins his realtor has lined up for him to see in the Land Between the Lakes area. He's thinking about getting a cabin that his whole family can use."

"The Land Between the Lakes? I've heard of that," Sarah responded. "It's between Lake Barkley and the Kentucky Lake, Isn't it? Sort of a recreational area?"

"The brochure he brought me called it a '170,000-acre playground,' but the surrounding towns have restaurants, hotels, and cabins, and that's where he's been looking. His girls and their families love hiking and boating. It sounds like a perfect spot where they can have family get-togethers. He doesn't get to see them very often."

"How far away is it from here?" Sarah asked, still in shock that her friend was planning to go away with Norman so early in their relationship.

"It's a little over four hours from here and, for your information," she added, puffing up indignantly, "he has arranged separate rooms for the two of us. I assume that's what's behind that look on your face."

"That look on my face is simply surprise. Tell me about his family. I haven't heard much about them." *I haven't heard much about him for that matter*, Sarah thought but didn't say.

"His wife died about ten years ago, and he has two daughters, both married with grown children. They live in Tennessee, south of the lakes, and he figures that area would be a perfect meeting place. They will all be there this weekend."

"Hmm," Sarah responded. "This is an interesting turn of events. …"

"Now Sarah, don't make more of this than it is."

"You're meeting the family. …"

"I know, but I'm trying to ignore that part."

"And you're leaving tomorrow?"

"This afternoon, actually," Sophie responded. "Will you help me pack?"

Chapter 3

Charles had just left for an appointment with his cardiologist and, being eager to get a look at her new neighbor's vintage fabric, Sarah headed for Bernice's house. A few minutes before 10:00, she knocked on the screen door but didn't get an answer right away. A minute or so later, she heard Bernice calling to her from the back of the house. "It's open, Sarah. Come on in."

Sarah stepped into the house that had once been her own, but it still didn't look familiar. The living room was sparsely furnished, but clean and tidy. The boxes from her previous visit were gone. She hesitated, not sure what to do next, but at that moment Bernice again called to her. "I'm sorry, Sarah. I had a phone call and got behind. I'll be with you in a jiffy."

Sarah started to sit down but heard Bernice add, "There's coffee brewing and mugs in the cabinet. Help yourself."

Sarah crossed the living room and stepped into the kitchen. Bernice had placed a small table and two chairs in the same spot where Sarah's table had been. For a moment Sarah hesitated, picturing herself and Charles sitting by the window, sipping coffee and getting to know one another.

She smiled remembering the warmth and excitement they had shared in those early days. She remembered feeling like a young girl instead of a seventy-year-old widow rediscovering love.

Shaking herself out of her reverie, Sarah automatically reached for a mug in the cabinet above the dishwasher and was not surprised to find that was exactly where Bernice kept them as well. She filled the mug with coffee and had just opened the refrigerator to get milk when Bernice came into the room.

"I was just getting some milk," Sarah explained, embarrassed by having been caught opening a stranger's refrigerator. "It just felt so natural. ..."

Bernice laughed. "It must feel strange to you being in the house you used to live in, but I'm glad that you feel comfortable enough to help yourself. There's half-and-half on the door if you prefer, or I have non-dairy creamer as well."

"This is fine," Sarah responded adding a few dollops of milk to her cup.

Bernice reached into the cupboard for a box of cookies and emptied a few onto a plate, which she sat on the table. "Sorry, but this is all I have to offer you. I need to do some shopping, but I want to get more of these boxes unpacked first."

"I'm going to the store this afternoon. Is there anything I can pick up for you?" Sarah asked as she sat down at the table and glanced across the street at Sophie's house.

"No, but thank you. Darius took my list and said he'd pick up what I need."

"Darius?" Sarah responded, hoping Bernice would explain who the young man was.

Bernice sank into a chair looking troubled. "Darius was my foster child. He left me when he was eighteen. That's when the agency released him from foster care. He comes back now and then when he needs help, and I just can't refuse him. He doesn't have anyone else. Yesterday he said he needed to borrow my car for a few hours, and I gave him the keys." Bernice sighed and took a sip of her coffee.

"And he hasn't returned?"

"No, but I'm sure he'll be along soon."

"Has he called?"

Bernice shook her head. "I tried to call him, but he didn't answer. He forgets to turn his phone on...."

Sarah was curious, but she didn't want to ask any more questions. Putting the issue of the car aside, the two women spent the next couple of hours in the bedroom that Sarah had used as her sewing room when she lived there. They started with several boxes of vintage fabrics that Bernice hadn't been able to part with and ended with one of the trunks of feedsacks. Sarah was fascinated by the patterns that reminded her of things from her childhood—quilts, clothing, even her grandmother's pieced tablecloths.

"I had no idea this was what my mother and grandmother were using," Sarah marveled, "but it's all very familiar to me. What are you planning to do with all this?"

"I have no idea," Bernice replied. "I sure don't have room for it here. Do you suppose I might be able to sell the feedsacks? I really don't know whether anyone would be interested."

"I know they would, Bernice. We should take a few to Running Stitches and talk to Ruth. If anyone knows what you could do with it, it would be Ruth."

"Running Stitches?"

"Oh, sorry. Running Stitches is our local quilt shop, and Ruth is the owner. I buy most of my fabric there. Oh," she added enthusiastically, "and we have a quilting group that meets there on Tuesday nights. Sophie and I go and would love to have you join us next week. You could show the group your feedsacks and perhaps get some ideas about what to do with them."

By the time Sarah was leaving, Bernice had agreed, at least tentatively, to join them the following Tuesday and bring some of the feedsacks to show the quilters.

"Thank you, Sarah," Bernice said at the door. "I was worried about moving to a retirement community and not knowing anyone. You and Sophie have made me feel very welcomed."

"You've met Sophie, so you'll never be lonely, I can assure you. When I moved here, Sophie swept me into her circle and had me running someplace every day and meeting more people than I'd known in my lifetime!"

Bernice laughed. "I'd like that. Thanks again, Sarah," she repeated as Sarah was walking away.

"Call me if you need anything," Sarah said as she was leaving. She was pleased that Bernice appeared more relaxed and seemed to have enjoyed the time they spent going through the fabric and feedsacks.

* * * * *

"Sophie called three times while you were out," Charles announced as she walked in the door.

"Why didn't she call my cell phone?" Sarah said with a frown in her voice.

"This cell phone?" her husband asked, holding up her phone which she had left on the kitchen counter.

"Oh, I forgot to put it in my purse again, didn't I?"

"I answered all of her calls on your behalf."

"Is she okay?" Sarah asked.

"She's fine. She just wants to tell you about some quilt museum they passed on the way down there."

"Tell me what Doctor Grossman had to say," Sarah said as casually as she could, trying not to let the anxiety she'd been feeling about her husband's health show in her voice. He'd had two serious strokes since he retired from the police department and his blood pressure had been running very high the past month despite several medication changes.

"Oh, you know how doctors are, sweetie. Lose weight, reduce stress, get exercise … I don't know what else I can do. I'm eating rabbit food and working out just about every day."

"Is that all he said?" She detected some hesitation in his voice, and she felt he wasn't telling the whole story. *I should have gone with him*, she told herself. "Charles, you might as well tell me and get it over with. You know how annoying I can be.…"

Charles laughed and put his arm around his wife. "You can be a bit of a nag, my dear wife, but I know you're just looking out for me."

"And what else did he say?" she asked again, not letting him off the hook.

"He's going to do a few tests next week."

"What kind of tests?"

"Something about the carotid artery.…"

"You had that last week," she responded, beginning to feel annoyed with herself for not going with him.

"This is different," he offered, realizing he'd better be more forthcoming with the details before she lost patience with him. "It's a … wait, I wrote it down here." He reached into his breast pocket and pulled out the doctor's appointment card. He turned it over and read, "It's a carotid angiography. He said he'd be inserting a catheter into an artery in the groin, insert dye, and do x-rays to see what's going on."

"When is your appointment?"

"They will be calling me once they get the test set up at the hospital."

"The hospital?" Sarah responded apprehensively but then realized that this sort of test would be done in the hospital. "Well, let me know when it is."

Sarah tried not to worry about Charles' health, but occasionally his symptoms would flare up, and she'd feel panicky. He was recovering from a massive stroke when she met him, but he worked hard and made a miraculous recovery. Since then, he'd suffered one other serious stroke and a few minor ones, none of which left him with any long-term effects.

Despite kidding her about the food she served him, Charles followed the doctor's instructions regarding exercise and diet, but it was against his nature to avoid stress. He continued to stay in touch with his old department and occasionally took on assignments from his lieutenant. He'd even been toying lately with getting licensed as a private investigator, but Sarah was dead set against it and, so far, he'd respected her wishes.

"Can we stop talking about this?" Charles said abruptly. "Tell me about your visit with Bernice."

"Well, I enjoyed going through the vintage fabrics. . . ." she replied hesitantly.

"But?" he responded, picking up on her ambivalence.

"Well, there's the car issue. . . ."

"She didn't get her car back yet?"

"Not yet," Sarah responded, and went on to tell Charles about Darius and his relationship to Bernice. "Bernice said he just borrowed it for a couple of days, but she hasn't heard from him since he left with the car and her grocery list."

"Is she worried?"

"If she is, she's keeping it to herself. But otherwise, she's all moved in, and the kitchen almost made me homesick. She has it arranged just like we did. Remember sitting at the table by the window? We were so much in love. . . ." she said smiling at him.

"I still am," Charles said emphatically, happy to see that she was getting off the subject of his health, "and I hope you are too. You are, aren't you?" he asked, pretending to be apprehensive about her answer.

"Of course, I am. But it's more of a settled-down love now. In those days I was giddy, and I think you were too!"

"I was," he admitted. "But don't ever tell my cop friends that," he added.

Chapter 4

"Hi, Sophie. How's the trip going?"

"So far, it's fantastic. I'm having such a good time, and the cabin he picked out is perfect. We drove around with the realtor this morning and looked at three or four nice ones, but when we pulled up in front of this one, I could tell it was going to be it. It's an entirely furnished A-frame with a loft, four bedrooms, and floor-to-ceiling windows facing the lake. There's a deck large enough to entertain the entire family at one time, and it has its own pier. It's a wooded lot, and it feels isolated, although there are other cabins not far away. It's so peaceful, Sarah. I really love it here."

"You're in the cabin now?"

"Yes, he was able to rent it for the weekend, but he's planning to buy it. He signed the contract yesterday, and he's already talked to his bank."

"And the family?"

"One daughter has arrived with her husband and their son. The son's in his thirties and not married. They seem nice. The older daughter will be here later today, but she's divorced, and neither of her kids could make this trip, but she's bringing her grandson.

"Norman's a great-grandfather?" Sarah exclaimed.

"He sure is, and it sounds like the whole family is excited about having the cabin. They live in Tennessee, and it's only about a two-hour drive for them. They seem like nice folks, but that's not why I called."

"So why did you call?" Sarah asked curiously.

"Norman and I stopped at the Visitor's Center to get brochures, and there was one about this museum, The National Quilt Museum in Paducah."

"Oh, Sophie, I hope you can spend some time there. I've heard it's an incredible collection of quilts."

"Norman said we could stay over an extra day and spend it at the museum. From the brochure, it looks fantastic. People come from all over the world to see their quilts. I probably don't know enough about quilts to really appreciate it, but I'm excited about going."

"I'm excited for you, and I wish I could be with you there. Take lots of pictures."

The two friends continued talking, and Sarah told her about the feedsacks and that Bernice might be going with them to the quilt club.

"Is the car back yet?" Sophie asked.

"Not yet, but it's okay. That was her grown foster son that we saw," Sarah responded, but decided not to pursue the topic and get Sophie worried. "She's almost completely settled in her new house," Sarah said as a way of changing the subject. "I can hardly wait for you to see the feedsacks. I know they'll remind you of your childhood."

* * * * *

"Sarah, it's Bernice." Sarah was glad to hear from her. It had been several days, and she was hoping the car had been returned. She'd been hesitant to call and ask, not wanting to be intrusive.

"I hate to ask this of you," Bernice continued, "but you were so kind to me the other day, and I don't know anyone else to call. I tried to reach Sophie, but there's no answer. Could you please come over?"

"Sophie's out of town for another day or two, but I'd be happy to come over. I was just getting ready to walk my dog. May I bring him?"

"Of course. Thank you, Sarah," she responded with a slight tremor in her voice.

"Do you want me to come with you?" Charles asked. Sarah had told him about the phone call and that Bernice sounded upset.

"I'll call you if I need you. She'd probably be more comfortable talking to me. And, before you ask, yes I have my cell phone!"

Bernice was again apologetic when Sarah arrived. "I shouldn't be bothering you with this. It's just that I've been so upset and I needed to talk to someone." As she was talking, she pulled two mugs out of the cupboard and filled them with coffee.

"Bernice, I know this isn't my business, but I see your car is still gone. Have you heard from Darius?"

"I haven't been able to reach him," Bernice responded. "My calls just go to the machine. I'm so worried, Sarah."

"Would you like for me to drive you over to his house so you can talk to him?"

"I don't know where he lives. He told me he was staying with some friends. Sarah, I think something has happened to him."

Sarah was baffled. She knew very little about Bernice and nothing about her situation. She didn't want to pry, but the woman seemed to be asking for help. "Does he have any family?"

"He was taken away from his family when he was ten years old and placed in foster care. By the time he came to me, he was thirteen, had been in several foster homes, and was an angry child."

"And his parents?"

"His father's in prison for life, and his mother was a prostitute back then. Since then she died. The social worker came one day to tell Darius about it."

"How did he take it?"

"He went out with his buddies and robbed a liquor store that night. He spent the next few months in detention, but they brought him back to me after that. I tried, Sarah, I really did. But that boy was so angry. I wondered if he'd been abused, but the agency wasn't allowed to share that information with me."

Sarah listened intently and wondered how this woman had been able to deal with all these problems from a child who wasn't even her own.

"He was arrested another couple of times before he was eighteen. I don't know what kind of trouble he might have gotten himself into now."

"How old is Darius?" Sarah asked.

"He's twenty-three."

"Did he have siblings that he might have gone to?"

"Not that I know of. He never mentioned any. I suspected there was a lot more to the story than I ever knew about, but I just tried to take it one day at a time and give him the love he never had. It probably helped some."

"I'm sure it did, Bernice. He was lucky to have you, and he still turns to you when he needs help."

Bernice dropped her eyes, looking embarrassed. "That's sort of what I wanted to talk to you about. I'm embarrassed to tell you this part, but he has emptied out my checking account."

"What?" Sarah exclaimed. "How was he able to do that, Bernice?" Sarah was beginning to wonder if Darius was physically abusive as well.

"He just went to the bank and withdrew it I guess."

"Is he on your account?"

"Yes," Bernice responded, again looking embarrassed. "He told me it would help him establish credit if he could show he had money in the bank." Bernice wasn't making eye contact, and Sarah knew there was much more to this story.

"Has he done this before?"

"Just small amounts and he'd always say he was going to pay me back, but he never did."

"Has he taken much this time?" Sarah asked.

"I just got off the phone with the bank. He's taken every penny out of the checking account. Of course, I still have my savings and my certificate. I'm afraid he'll figure out a way to get those too."

"Well, I know one thing we can do," Sarah responded, determined to help her new friend. "We can go to the bank and close your account so he can't get his hands on any more of your money. We'll open a new account in just your name. Would that be okay?"

"I guess so. There's money from the state too, my pension," Bernice said. "I'll have to find the paperwork...."

"Let's go to the bank and talk with the manager. I'm sure he can arrange for your next check to go into the new account until you can get your direct deposits changed. We can let him know what has happened so he can be on the lookout if Darius tries something like this again. Okay?"

"But what about Darius? I don't know what has happened to him."

Sarah sighed. The boy had been financially exploiting his foster mother, and yet she's more concerned about his welfare than her own.

"Let's deal with one problem at a time, Bernice. Let's get the bank issue solved, and then we'll talk to my husband. He's a retired police detective ..."

"Oh no," Bernice wailed. "No police. Darius told me to never talk to the police about him. But now I just don't know, Sarah. How could he do this to me?"

"Bernice, let's go to the bank and get your finances secure, and then let's go out to lunch. I want to show you our quilt shop, and there's a lovely little café right across the street from it. We can talk there."

Sarah was pleased to see her new neighbor begin to relax and, as a smile began to form on her face, Bernice said, "Let's take a few feedsacks with us and talk to your friend."

She's going to be able to deal with this, Sarah told herself with a sigh of relief.

* * * * *

"The guy's got more than a juvie record," Charles announced as he walked into Sarah's sewing room the next morning.

"What?"

"He's been arrested twice in the past year for grand theft auto. Some sleazy lawyer over on the East Side got him off the first time, and he was awaiting trial on the second. Your friend didn't tell you about that?"

"I honestly don't think she knows. She seems to be under the impression that he's just a little down on his luck."

"This guy has created his own luck, and it isn't good."

"Wait. Earlier you said he was awaiting trial. If he doesn't turn up before the trial, she can see him there. When is it scheduled?"

"That trial was set for last week, and he never showed up. There's a bench warrant out for his arrest."

"Maybe that's where he is, in jail," Sarah responded.

"Nope. The first place I looked."

"Poor Bernice. Do you think I should tell her?"

"I don't know how she'd feel about us poking around in their business, but if you want to tell her, I'll go with you."

"She doesn't want to talk to you. ..."

"Me? Why?"

"Darius told her to stay away from the police."

"And that wasn't a red flag to this woman?"

"She's been in denial about this boy, Charles, but I think she's beginning to see the light. Emptying out her checking account seemed to get her attention," Sarah responded.

"He's no boy," Charles corrected. "He's a twenty-three-year-old criminal, and I hope he doesn't show up on her doorstep when he discovers the account has been closed."

"You think he's dangerous?" Sarah asked, aghast at the thought that her new friend might be in danger.

"I don't know, but Bernice needs to be prepared for that possibility."

"I doubt very much that she would agree with you."

Sarah was right. Presented with the idea later that day, Bernice was shocked that anyone could think her foster son could be a danger to anyone, especially to her.

She doesn't seem to realize that his financial exploitation of her was already placing her at risk. Sarah decided not to tell her about the warrant. Charles said the police would certainly be contacting her about it. Reluctantly, Sarah returned home, instructing Bernice to call if anything changed.

* * * * *

"I tried to wait until I got home to tell you about the museum, but I can't control myself," Sophie said when Sarah answered the phone.

"You and Norman were able to go?"

"We sure were, and Sarah, you and I are coming back here on our own. For one thing, Norman wanted to move through it much faster than I did. He didn't understand that it took me time to figure out these quilts. Most of them aren't like the ones we do in our club."

"What do you mean?"

"They are mostly very modern. 'Contemporary,' Norman called them. They are more like the pieces we saw in the art museum in Hamilton. Even the Log Cabin designs are all catawampus, but they are beautiful, and some quilts looked like photographs from a distance—landscapes, buildings reflected in the water. And the colors! They are exquisite. I can't imagine how they did them, and I can hardly wait to come back down here with you. You'll love it!"

"Nothing traditional?" Sarah asked.

"Oh yes! I saw traditional ones too, and some from the 1800s, but I think those might have been special exhibits. Most of the quilts that the museum displays are award winners from around the country. Like I said, Norman was rushing me, but I saw some that looked like they'd taken traditional patterns and put them into more modern settings. You'll see when we go."

"I hope you took lots of pictures."

"Oh my, I forgot to tell you. Visitors aren't permitted to take photographs in the museum. Sorry, but you promised you'd come back here with me, so you'll be able to see them firsthand, which will be much better anyway."

"Well Sophie, I actually thought about the fact that your picture taking needs work anyway."

"And just what does that mean," Sophie responded indignantly. Sarah could imagine her friend all puffed up with her fists on her hips.

"It's just that the pictures you took at Martha's wedding …"

"Are you referring to the fact that I got pictures of everyone's shoes but not their heads?"

"That's exactly what I was referring to."

"Humph," Sophie replied, but added, "I guess I see your point. So you'll come back down with me?"

"You bet I will. I can hardly wait," Sarah assured her friend excitedly.

"Soon?"

"Yes, very soon."

"Norman said it'll take you and me a little over three hours from Middletown to Paducah, so I thought we might make a mini-vacation of it and stay over."

"That sounds like fun," Sarah responded, catching her friend's enthusiasm.

"And the brochure says they have a quilt show here every year and people come from all over the country," Sophie continued.

"Oh yes! I've heard about that show, and I'd love to go," Sarah responded excitedly. "In fact, Ruth said she might get a bus trip organized for next year."

"But I want you and me to go on our own before that," Sophie insisted. "You never should have talked me into quilting, Sarah. You've created a monster!"

"But a likable one," Sarah laughed, enjoying her friend's enthusiasm. "See you soon."

"We'll be home late. We're stopping for dinner on the way."

"And you had a good time at the lake?"

"Absolutely. Come for coffee in the morning, and I'll tell you all about it.

When she hung up, Sarah saw that Charles was smiling. "I notice you didn't mention Bernice," he said.

"I didn't want to bring her down. She sounds very happy."

Chapter 5

"I see you brought a guest this week, Sarah. Would you introduce her to the group?" Ruth had met Bernice the previous week when Sarah brought her into Running Stitches to talk about the feedsacks, but she wanted Sarah to make the introductions to the quilt group.

"This is my new neighbor, Bernice Jenkins. Bernice is a quilter, and she has something very unique to tell us about.

Bernice had brought a large tote bag filled with feedsacks which she pulled out as soon as they had gone around the room introducing Bernice to all the members. She began by telling the group how she had come to own this collection of feedsacks.

"Why are they called feedsacks?" Caitlyn asked. Caitlyn, at seventeen, was the youngest member of the group and daughter of Andy, Sarah and Sophie's close friend.

"I'm still learning about them," Bernice responded, "but I do know my father would bring these bags home filled with feed for the farm animals when I was a child."

"And bulk items for the kitchen came in these bags, too, like sugar and flour," Delores added. Delores was the oldest member and the most experienced quilter.

"You're right, those came in these same bags," Bernice responded. "Times were hard, and fabric was scarce in those days, and being frugal, the farmer's wives would use the bags to make things for the family."

At first, Bernice held up the plain muslin ones which displayed the name of the company. "As you can see," she said, "at first they were white and had the company logo printed on them and the farmers' wives couldn't use them for outerwear, but they would make dishrags, diapers, and even undergarments for the whole family." She passed the bags around, and the group talked about the different things that could be made from them.

"When the companies realized that women were using them for sewing, they started printing them in pretty colors and made their labels removable," she said as she pulled out several bright solid-colored bags, "and later they began to add patterns like these." The group oohed and aahed as she pulled out sack after sack in colorful florals, stripes, and plaids.

Sarah and Sophie looked at one another and smiled, both pleased to see the progress their new friend had made in the past few days. She'd been through a great deal. Her car had not been returned, she hadn't heard from her foster son, and the police had been hounding her about his whereabouts. She'd been forced to face the truth about the young man that she'd invested so much of herself in over the years.

"I have a trunk full of my grandmother's things made with vintage fabrics, and many of those items were made from feedsacks," Delores said, smiling as she reminisced. "She made all the children's dresses, our curtains, anything that required fabric. I remember she told me that it took three matching feedsacks to make a dress for herself, and sometimes my grandfather had to buy seeds he didn't even want in order to get the right feedsacks for her." Everyone chuckled.

Pulling several more feedsacks from her tote bag, Bernice said, "Now these are examples of a smart marketing tool the feed companies came up with a little later." She held up feedsacks with printed teddy bears and dolls. "The women would just cut these out and stitch them together for their children."

"I think we have a doll just like that one in the attic," Kimberly cried, looking at her sister.

"You may be right," Christina replied thoughtfully. "We should look for it. I wonder whether mother or granny made it."

"We'll never know," Kimberly responded sadly. "Mother tried to tell us so many stories those last few months, but we were just so busy with her care. …"

"I think we all have regrets," Delores interjected. "There are so many things I wish I had asked Mother, and I know there were times she was telling me stories from her past and I was only half listening."

"There are stories I'd like to share with my children," Sarah added, "memories that are going to be lost forever if they aren't told, but our kids are busy, and truth be known, I don't think today's generation are really that interested in bygone days."

"I took a class once," Delores added, "about the stages of life we all go through, and they stressed the importance of listening to our elders when they want to tell these stories. Their stage of life is all about life review—making sense of it all—and telling their stories is an important part of doing that."

The group remained quiet for a few moments, each thinking about what Delores had said.

"Okay Girls," Sophie announced abruptly. "This is becoming way too solemn for my taste. I want to hear more from Bernice."

The group seemed to appreciate that Sophie had lightened the mood as they all turned toward Bernice with anticipation.

"I don't have much more to say," Bernice confessed. "I just wanted to show them to you and to get your opinion on something. I was hoping you folks might have an idea of what I can do with these. I'd like to get them out of my house since I have three large steamer trunks sitting in the middle of a room that could be my sewing room. Sarah and Sophie suggested that you might have some ideas."

"Three trunks full?" Allison gasped. Allison was a young mother who had been a knitter but turned to quilting when she discovered Ruth's shop and the quilt group.

"Well," Kimberly began, "I've seen them for sale online, but they're usually pretty expensive, and I have no idea what the demand would be." Kimberly and her sister, Christina, owned a long-arm quilting machine and did most of the quilting for members of the group.

Her sister spoke up saying, "Yes, but I've also seen feed-sacks for sale as pre-cut fabric, like charm packs."

"Charm packs?" Caitlyn asked. Caitlyn being a new quilter had very little experience shopping for fabrics.

"Five-inch squares sold in a bundle," Ruth responded. She walked around the corner and brought back a charm pack for Caitlyn to see. "They also come in ten-inch squares called layer cakes."

"Would you be willing to cut your feedsacks up?" Ruth asked, turning to Bernice.

"I guess so," Bernice responded thoughtfully. "It never occurred to me."

"But I don't know about limiting the size to charm packs," Ruth added. "I'd be inclined to offer them in packages of four-inch, five-inch, and six-inch pieces. That would meet most people's needs, I would think."

"There'll be waste if she starts cutting them up that way," Allison remarked.

"Then she can also offer scrap bags."

"I like this idea," Bernice responded, "but where would I sell them?"

"You could get a website, I guess," Anna suggested. "My husband could help you set it up." Anna was Ruth's sister, and her husband had been responsible for setting up Ruth's online business. Sarah noticed that Bernice was frowning, and she figured the idea of maintaining a website didn't appeal to her.

"I have an idea," Ruth said. "I've signed up for a table at the Hamilton Quilt Show next month. I'd be happy to give you one end of my booth, and you could sell packets there."

Bernice looked interested, but responded, "Once I start cutting these up and packaging them, there could be hundreds of packets. Do you think I should get my own booth?"

"That's a good idea," Delores responded. "I have a couple of feedsack quilts in that trunk in my attic. We could hang them in your booth as examples of how they could be used.

I could even bring a couple of aprons and maybe a child's dress to display as well."

"I think I'm going to start cutting!" Bernice announced enthusiastically. "This sounds like fun."

"I'd like to put in my order for a few packets of four-inch pieces," Sarah said, and immediately three other members called out their own orders.

"I'd like to put an assortment of them right here in the shop," Ruth said. "Once you get your pricing figured out, come see me, and I'll buy a few of each size."

"I may not have enough for a booth by the time I finish cutting the orders I got tonight," Bernice joked as they drove home after the meeting.

"Do you want any help with the cutting?"

"That's a very kind offer. I'll let you know, but in the meantime, this is a great project for keeping my mind off Darius' problems."

Maybe it isn't much, Sarah thought, *but she's thinking of it as Darius' problem and not her own. That's progress.*

* * * * *

"Sarah, it's Bernice. I need to ask you a question. Is this a good time?"

Sarah and Charles had just sat down to lunch, but Bernice sounded eager to speak with her, so she told her it was fine.

"I just had a call from Ruth. She said she'd been talking to the coordinator of the Hamilton Quilt Show to find out if it was possible for me to get a booth at this late date, and the woman said I could, but she also was very interested in the feedsacks. She said one of her speakers has canceled, and they're looking for someone to do a short presentation, and she wondered if I would do it. What do you think? I have no idea what I'd say. ..."

"Bernice, this sounds like an excellent opportunity, and you can start by saying exactly what you said at the meeting Tuesday night. You gave a fascinating presentation, and everyone was excited about it. Sophie and I can help if you'd like."

"Would you sit up front with me?"

"Sure, and we can even take turns talking if that would make you more comfortable, and we can help you handle the booth too if you'd like."

"That would make me feel so much better, Sarah. Thank you," Bernice responded gratefully. "Ruth said there'd be no charge for the booth if I do the presentation," Bernice added, sounding reluctantly excited. "And you really think I should do this?"

"Absolutely," Sarah responded.

After a short pause, Bernice exclaimed, "I'm calling her back right now."

* * * * *

"What are you making?" Charles asked a couple of days later as he stepped into the sewing room where Sarah was using her rotary cutter and a template to cut six-sided pieces of fabric.

"I'm making a wall hanging with the scraps of fabric that Bernice gave me yesterday while we were cutting. She held up a magazine with a picture of a quilt square which had been displayed in a round, wooden frame.

"I hope you aren't going to ask me to make that round frame."

"It's not actually a frame. It's an embroidery hoop, but I found this picture, and I think, with Sophie's help with the hand work, I can make hexagons from these scraps and put them in a hoop like this person did with her quilt square."

Charles looked at her blankly for a moment, not understanding what she meant, but finally nodded and said, "That will be nice."

Sarah laughed knowing he had no idea what she had in mind. "You'll see it soon. It's for the new guest room."

"The *new* guest room?" he responded as his eyebrows shot up his forehead. "Did I miss something?"

"I was going to talk to you about it once I got it clear in my head. What I have in mind is redecorating the guest room in a vintage style to go with my grandmother's spindle bed. I saw an antique wash basin and pitcher at the antique shop in Hamilton. I think I'll go back and buy that and put it on the antique dresser with one of my old embroidered dresser scarves under it."

Looking a bit lost as he tried to picture what his wife was talking about, he responded simply, "Sounds nice too."

Sarah sighed, shook her head, and continued cutting out her hexagons. "You'll see," she said to his back as he was leaving the room.

Chapter 6

"Charles, I have another idea."

"Let's hear it," Charles responded as he stretched out on the lounge chair in the backyard. It was a warm, sunny morning with signs of spring popping up everywhere. He'd been working on the household budget and decided to bring his project outside with Sarah and enjoy the day.

Sarah had been preparing her flower beds all morning and appeared to be having problems with her back when she stood. "Why don't you come sit down with me for a few minutes and rest your back," he added.

She leaned back, stretching her back with a relieved sigh, pulled off her gardening gloves, and joined him. "Is this for me?" she asked, seeing the second glass of iced tea on the small table between them.

"It is," he said. "So, tell me about your idea."

"Okay, well as you know Bernice is selling feedsack fabric, and I need a bedspread for the redecorated guest room. A vintage one would be perfect."

"I see. So what do you have in mind?"

"I'd like to purchase enough four-inch squares from Bernice to make a vintage quilt for Grandmother's spindle bed."

"You don't need my permission, sweetie."

"I know, but I wanted to run it by you since it is going to involve more money than I usually spend on a quilt. These vintage feedsacks aren't priced like cotton on the bolt."

Sarah asked to use the notebook and pen that Charles had brought outside with him. He turned to a blank page and handed it to her along with the pen, and she quickly sketched what she had in mind. She drew a row of four-patch blocks and told him they would each be made with different pieces of feedsack fabric to give it a scrappy look. "I'll separate the blocks with a solid sashing and probably add cornerstones." She stopped talking when she realized her husband's eyes were glazing over.

"You'll see," she added as she closed the notebook and handed it back to him.

"That will be nice," he responded, having no idea what she was proposing. "Just go ahead and pick out the ones you want while you have lots to choose from." *He might not understand about quilt design*, she told herself with a smile, *but he sure understands about supply and demand, and I fully intend to choose mine before the show.*

After lunch, Sarah headed up the street to help Bernice package and price the fabric they had cut the previous day. As soon as they got settled down at the worktable, she asked Bernice if she could go ahead and purchase a couple dozen packets so that she could begin working on her quilt.

"Take as many as you want, Sarah, but I certainly won't charge you considering all the work you've done for me!"

"Bernice, I'm having a wonderful time doing this, and if there's one thing quilters can always count on, it's the help of fellow quilters. Now, I'm writing a check for twenty packages, and tomorrow I'll drive you to the bank to deposit it."

"Oh, you haven't heard," Bernice responded excitedly. "Norman is on his way over with one of his business vehicles. He's loaning it to me until Darius brings my car back."

"Fantastic. I wonder what it will be. He picked us up in a brand new Mercedes."

"It's a Volvo, but an older one he told me apologetically," Bernice sniggered. "I'll just be happy to be driving again. I've hated having to ask you folks to drive me around all the time."

"We've enjoyed it, but I'm glad he's helping out. I'm beginning to really like the man, and I think he's very good for Sophie."

"I couldn't say since I didn't know her before, but she sure seems happy," Bernice responded.

Within a couple of hours, Sarah and Bernice had packaged and priced dozens of packets in various sizes, including several scrap bags and the ones that Sarah had purchased.

"Now, what I need is fabric for the sashing," Sarah said.

"We could probably do something with the solid-colored sacks, but," Bernice continued, "I think you might like using a 1930s reproduction fabric in a solid color. What do you think?"

"Hmm. It sounds like it might work. Do you want to take a break and run over to Running Stitches so I can lay some of these pieces out on the 1930s fabrics?"

"Let's go," Bernice responded enthusiastically, sticking the check into her purse." It will give us a chance to try out that shiny silver car sitting in my driveway." While they had been working, Norman had dropped off the car.

They called Sophie to see if she wanted to go with them but learned she was on her way out with Norman.

When they arrived at the quilt shop, they were barely able to get a nod from Ruth. The shop was inundated with customers who were picking out their fabrics for a class that Delores was conducting. "We're fine," Sarah called to Ruth as she and Bernice headed for the reproduction fabrics.

"I think that green would go beautifully with the feed-sack fabrics," Bernice commented as Sarah held her samples against the various bolts of solid color fabric she had pulled out. Sarah moved her samples over to the green that Bernice was indicating and spread them out.

"It does look good," Sarah responded. "It doesn't compete with the patterns and even seems to make them pop." She lifted the bolt and read from the end label, "It's called celadon green, and it's a 1930s reproduction fabric. I just wish the whole quilt could be made with the feedsack fabric."

"I think this is as close as you'll get to the authenticity you want."

"Yes, I think this will work just fine," Sarah finally declared, standing back and looking at the bolt with her samples spread out on it. "I've been thinking about putting wallpaper in that room to help with the vintage look, and I'm sure I can find a floral that picks up this green." She pulled out her calculator and her notepad and began calculating what she'd need for the sashing and binding. "I think I'll put it on the back as well so that no other colors will be competing with the feedsacks."

"Excellent idea," Ruth said as she walked up. Sarah had been in the shop earlier in the week and had told her about her plans for the vintage guest room. "How big is your bed?" she asked as she ran her fingers over the feedsack patterns.

"It's an antique and what they called a three-quarter bed," Sarah responded. "It belonged to my grandmother, and people must have been smaller in those days, or they just wanted to snuggle," she added with a grin. "It's very narrow by today's standards. In fact, I had to special order the mattress." Flipping back through the pages of her notebook, she said, "It's forty-eight inches by seventy-five inches and will need about a fourteen-inch drop since we ordered a very thick mattress for it."

"Do you want a pillow tuck?" Ruth asked, pulling out her calculator.

"I think so. That will make the room look the way rooms looked back in the 30s."

"I agree," Ruth said as she pulled out her calculator and figured out what she recommended for the back. Sarah added the extra she would need for the sashing and binding and told Ruth she was ready to have the fabric cut.

In the meantime, Bernice was looking at a 1930s coral fabric. Since she still didn't have enough room to set up her sewing machine, Sophie had given her a quick lesson in English paper piecing, and she was working on a throw for her living room. She had chosen some of her favorite feedsack fabrics and was using Sophie's largest hexagon templates.

"I think this coral would be ideal for the back and the binding," she said as she picked up the bolt and followed

Ruth and Sarah to the cutting table. "I'd like to have Darius paint the living room a soft coral when he gets back," she added, more to herself than anyone else.

The women chatted about their plans and ultimately ended up at the cash register. "I'm sorry, Bernice. This card was declined," Ruth said, handing the credit card back to her. "Do you have another?"

"Declined? Did they say why?" Bernice asked, looking puzzled.

"No, they don't say why, but I'd be glad to try again if you think there's a mistake."

"There certainly is a mistake. I don't even have an amount due on that card. I pay it off every month." She handed the card back to Ruth, but it was again declined.

"I'm sorry, Bernice," Ruth said, feeling embarrassed for Sarah's friend.

"Well, I have a backup card. Let me find it." Bernice unzipped an inside pocket and pulled out another card. She checked the expiration dates on both cards, and they were current. "Here, this one will certainly work. I use it mostly for online purchases, but I pay it off every month, too."

They waited while Ruth again processed the sale, but looked up at Bernice and gently shook her head. "I'm sorry, Bernice. You should contact your bank right away."

The color had drained from Bernice's face as she contemplated what might be wrong. "You don't suppose …" but she didn't finish the sentence. "No, it can't be Darius this time. He doesn't have my cards." She reached into her purse and pulled out her wallet and handed Ruth cash. "This won't be declined," she said, attempting to make light of the situation.

Sarah knew Bernice was worried about what might have happened, and Sarah was far less confident about Darius' lack of complicity.

On their way home, Sarah asked Bernice if she still wanted to get together later in the afternoon to cut feedsacks and prepare packets for the show.

"I'm going to make some calls, but I'm not going to let this ruin my day," Bernice responded, much more chipper than she had been a few minutes earlier. "Sophie is coming over around 2:00. I'll call the credit card companies, but I'm sure there is some kind of mistake, probably involving my move."

"I'm sure you're right," Sarah reassured her, hoping her voice didn't convey the doubt she was feeling.

"Come on over around 2:00," Bernice called to her friend as she dropped Sarah off at her house. "This is all going to work out," she added with tenuous confidence.

As Sarah approached her front door, she saw Charles and Barney returning from the dog park. "Come on in," Sarah called to her husband. "I have an interesting development to tell you about while we have a quick lunch. I'm heading back to Bernice's house to cut fabric this afternoon."

As they ate, Sarah caught him up on the happenings of the morning. He pinched his lips and shook his head in disgust. "I totally agree with you. It was that no-good foster son of hers. He's found another way to rip her off. Did she say whether she gave him permission to use the card?"

"She said that she let him use them a couple of times just before she moved, but that he returned them right away and only made the few charges they'd agreed on at the time.

She's sure he had nothing to do with this, and that it's just a mistake."

"After ripping off her bank account and stealing her car, she still trusts him?" Charles replied incredulously.

"I think she knows. She's just not ready to admit it."

"So what's she going to do about the credit cards?"

She's calling the credit card companies now."

"Companies? More than one?"

"Yes, both of her cards were declined."

"That doesn't sound like a simple mistake to me, Sarah. Not if it happened with more than one company."

"I agree," she replied regretfully. "Another thing for Bernice to worry about."

"Another nail in Darius' coffin, if you ask me," Charles replied.

* * * * *

"This whole thing is very odd," Bernice was saying as Sarah arrived. Sophie was already there, and Bernice was catching her up on what had happened at the quilt shop.

"You called the companies?" Sarah asked as she took her jacket off and hung it on the hook in the entryway. Her mind flashed to that being the hook she had used for Barney's leash when he first came to live with her. She smiled remembering how he quickly learned to pull it down and drag it to her feet when he wanted to go for a walk.

"I called both companies, and they both said the same thing! The cards have been maxed out."

"What?"

"It's true. They both referred me to their fraud depart-ment, and they will both be calling me back as soon as they have a chance to go over the accounts. I still think it must be a mistake."

"How do you suppose it could have happened?" Sophie asked, but then looked at Sarah and immediately knew what her friend was thinking. *Darius strikes again.*

Sarah didn't want to state the obvious and remained silent. She could tell by the stiffness in Bernice's body and the tightness of her jaw, that she knew exactly what had happened, but just wasn't ready to admit it to her friends, and possibly not even to herself.

"Let's start cutting," Bernice announced abruptly. "The show is only a few weeks away, and we have two trunks we haven't even touched."

Chapter 7

"Do you want to come over for lunch?" Sarah asked when Sophie answered the phone a few days later. "I have my squares of feedsack fabric arranged, and I'd like for you to look at them before I start sewing them into four-patches."

"Is this for the quilt or the wall hanging?" Sophie asked.

"For the quilt. For the wall hanging, I'm just putting hexagons together randomly, but the quilt is going to be four-patch blocks separated by sashing, and I'm not sure whether to have all four fabrics different in each block or maybe have two sets of two matching fabrics. So, are you coming?"

"Sure," Sophie responded. "Is Bernice coming too?"

"I called her, but she wants to stay close to the phone. She's expecting calls from both of the credit card companies."

"I saw a police car there again this morning," Sophie stated.

"Yes," Sarah replied. "The credit card companies wanted her to report the incident to the police. She called the officer who's been asking her about Darius."

"Is she going to tell the police that she suspects Darius?"

"No, I don't think she even does, Sophie. She's blind to that young man's criminal behavior. She told me that when the officer advised her to report her car as stolen, she was furious!"

"I'll bet she was," Sophie responded. "I referred to it as stolen one day and I could tell she didn't like hearing that at all."

"He coming to take her statement today," Sarah said. "The poor woman ..."

"I feel bad for her, but I hope she's beginning to see the light. That boy is no good," Sophie added.

"I agree."

"So," Sophie announced, eager to change the subject to something lighter, "I'll be right over, and I'm bringing dessert."

Sarah had been going to the gym every couple of days, trying desperately to take off the few pounds she had gained over the winter and hopefully get her cholesterol down at the same time. "Something small, please, Sophie. You know I'm trying to lose weight."

"Nonsense," her cheerfully rotund friend replied. "You could stand to gain a few pounds if you ask me. A nurse once told me that we should all carry enough extra weight to handle a serious illness without wasting away."

"I don't think any one of us need to worry about wasting away, but go ahead and bring a little something sweet. I'm only serving salad, and Charles brought fresh croissants from the bakery."

"Okay," Sophie replied. "Start chopping up the rabbit food, and I'm on my way with the real deal." Sarah heard the sound of Sophie's timer ding and Sophie opening the oven door. She could imagine the smell of the freshly baked treat wafting through Sophie's kitchen.

After relaxing over lunch and talking about their plans to go to the museum, Sarah led Sophie to the sewing room where she had the four-inch feedsack squares spread out on her worktable. "Right now I have four different fabrics in each four-patch, but I tried to choose two light ones and two darker ones."

"And you've placed them opposite one another in each four-patch," Sophie noted. "I like the way you've arranged them," she added as she reached across the table and changed two or three of them. "I was amazed when I first saw Bernice's feedsacks," she continued. "I thought they'd be sort of clunky looking since they were used to transport animal feed."

"No, the manufacturers were competing for sales, so the patterns were often really delightful florals. Look at these red ones with white and yellow flowers."

"The patterns are very old-fashioned looking. I think I've seen some of these in the distant past, maybe at my grandmother's house," Sophie added. "They make me feel sort of melancholy."

"I know what you mean."

"This will be beautiful, and you're going to put this on the bed in your guest room?"

"That's the plan. Do you want to go antique shopping with me this week? I want to look at that antique wash bowl and pitcher I was telling you about."

"Sure. Sounds like fun."

* * * * *

"Look at this," Sarah exclaims. "Isn't this unique? And it matches my grandmother's spindle bed." It was several days later, and the two friends had decided to take the day off from cutting with Bernice and do some shopping. Sophie looked where Sarah was pointing and saw a slender, vintage two-shelf oak washstand with spindles connecting the shelves. The top shelf had a cutout and held a ceramic wash bowl and pitcher, and there was a towel bar on either side of the shelf. A mirror was attached to the stop of the stand, and the bottom shelf held an antique ceramic chamber pot.

"This is an all-in-one portable bathroom," Sophie commented just as the shopkeeper walked up.

"Lovely piece isn't it?" he said, seeing the enthusiasm on his customer's face.

"It would definitely match the room. I was thinking of buying a simple pitcher and wash bowl, but this would be even better. What are you asking for it?" Sarah asked.

"The stand itself is hand tooled and probably made in the late 1800s." He quoted the price, and Sarah agreed that it was probably reasonable for what she would be getting.

"Of course, the pitcher and bowl are priced separately."

"Oh," Sarah responded, looking disappointed but went ahead and asked for the price of those items as well.

"And the chamber pot?" Sophie asked.

"I'd be willing to throw that in if you purchase the other items."

"Generous," Sophie responded in that sarcastic tone that Sarah sometimes found annoying, but this time seemed appropriate.

Sarah thanked the man and headed for the door with Sophie right behind her. "Can you imagine having the nerve to ask that price?" she said once they were outside.

"I know," Sophie responded. "It's outrageous."

"I think I'm going to buy it," Sarah announced and Sophie stopped in her tracks.

"You're kidding!"

"It's perfect for the room, Sophie. It exactly matches the bed and will look excellent with the feedsack quilt."

"I wonder what Charles will have to say about this?" Sophie replied.

"I'll call him now. Let's go sit down in that restaurant over there and have lunch."

"Chinese! Oh, good."

After they had placed their orders, Sarah dialed the number and chatted with her husband before getting around to the issue. When she began describing the washstand, he questioned the need for more furniture, and she explained the size and how perfectly it went with the room. Sarah was quiet, and Sophie figured Charles was speaking. Finally, Sarah spoke again saying, "The price? Well, I haven't added it up, but it's somewhere in the neighborhood of $600 altogether." She frowned as she listened to his response. Finally, she said, "Okay, I'll try, but this will probably squelch the deal." She looked disappointed.

Hanging up the phone just as their meal arrived, she turned to Sophie and said, "He wants me to offer $500."

"He'll never accept that," Sophie responded.

"I know, but it's worth a try."

A few hours later, Sarah and Sophie were loading the wash basin and all the accouterments into the car. "It worked!" Sophie exclaimed.

"Well, he wouldn't give us the chamber pot, but the price for that piece was pretty reasonable."

When she returned home, Sarah stood in the guest room and looked around. In her mind, she could imagine the room finished with a soft floral wallpaper in shades of green and pale yellow. Suddenly she realized what she had done. "This is my room at my grandmother's house," she exclaimed.

"What sweetie?" she heard Charles call from his computer room.

"This room," she said as he came in, "it's going to be just like the room I slept in when I visited my grandmother in Indiana."

"How old were you then?"

"Oh, I was around six or seven the first time I went there alone, but I went every summer until I was in high school and my friends became more important to me than family. You remember how that was."

"Boys aren't as much like that, I guess. We became interested in sports and stopped wanting to hang around with family much earlier." They sat down in the guest room while Sarah pointed out where she would be placing the furniture and described the wallpaper which he had agreed to help her hang. The room was causing childhood memories to come flooding back, and they remained sitting and talking until dinnertime.

"I had no idea I was reproducing a memory," Sarah said as they stood.

"These are the smallest chairs I ever sat in," Charles complained as he struggled to straighten up in a standing position.

"They are boudoir chairs, Charles. They're supposed to be small."

"They certainly achieved that," he complained as they headed up the hall toward the kitchen. "And I'm hungry," he added.

Chapter 8

It was nearly midnight when Charles' cell phone rang. He glanced at the screen and recognized Matt Stokely's cell number. Lieutenant Matthew Stokely was Charles' superior when he was with the department and a very close friend since his retirement.

"I'll take this in the den," he said, not wanting to interrupt the end of the movie Sarah was watching. When he returned to the living room much later, the movie had ended, and Sarah was gathering up the magazines she'd been thumbing through during the commercials.

"Has Bernice mentioned hearing anything from her foster son?" he asked.

"Not a word. Why do you ask?"

"Well, that was Matt on the phone, and there's been a development."

"A development?" Sarah asked, laying her magazines aside. "What kind of development?"

"They found your friend's car."

"That's wonderful," she exclaimed. "Bernice will be so pleased," but then she noticed the serious look on her husband's face and her enthusiasm waned. "And Darius? Did they find him too? Is he okay?"

"No word on him yet, but his fingerprints were all over the car. Matt said it looked like he'd been living in it."

"Where did they find it?"

"Just outside Nashville," Charles responded.

"Tennessee? What was he doing all the way down there?" Sarah asked.

"No idea."

"Will they return the car to Bernice?"

"Not right away. It's probably going to be impounded for the time being until they complete the investigation."

"Why do they need to investigate? He didn't steal the car, Charles. She handed him the keys and said he could use it." Sarah was confused about why the car would be important to the police.

Charles hadn't told her about the body in the trunk.

* * * * *

"It doesn't feel right keeping this from Sarah," Charles was saying. It was the following morning, and he was sitting across the desk from Matt Stokely in the Middletown police station.

"You remember how it was, Charlie," Matt responded. "You were our star detective and were assigned the hottest cases we had back in the day, but you knew when to hold things close to the vest. We don't want the press getting their hands on the details yet. That girl was the daughter of an influential politician, and we don't know just what we're dealing with here. The car was found nearly four hundred miles from here, just south of Nashville."

"I know, Matt, but Sarah is very close to Darius' foster mother and …"

"That's just it, Charles. She was his foster mother. If we were talking about the young man's parents or even his siblings, it would be different, but we don't owe anything to an ex-foster parent, no matter how close they've become. And it's not as if we're withholding information about him. We sent a patrolman over last night and let her know that we found the car. And the press has already run with the fact that Councilman Waterford's daughter is dead. We just haven't announced any details about where the body was found."

"Do you suspect Darius of murdering the girl?"

"We don't know that. We certainly know he was in the car at some point, but we don't know where he is, and we don't have any other leads. Are you willing to talk to the detective about what you know?"

"Sure, but Sarah and Darius' foster mother know much more than I do. You should be talking to them."

"We will in time."

* * * * *

The phone rang just as Sarah was scooping oatmeal into her bowl. Charles had already left to meet with his friend and ex-supervisor Matt Stokely at the police station. She wiped her hands and reached for it, surprised to see Bernice's name on the display this early. "Good morning, Bernice," she said cheerfully.

The line was quiet for a moment, then her friend spoke with a trembling voice. "They found the car all the way down in Tennessee."

"I know, Bernice. Charles told me late last night. I'm so glad."

"But they aren't going to return it to me."

"Did they say why?"

"They stated that they'd let me know later in the week. Mostly they were just questioning me about Darius' where-abouts and asking me those same questions they keep asking. I don't think they believe me that I don't know where he is. He must be in more trouble than just the bench warrant. There was a police car sitting out front all night just watching the house.

"I'll be right over," Sarah responded. She called Sophie and told her to meet her at Bernice's right away. "They found the car, and she's worried sick about Darius. The police are hounding her about his whereabouts."

"I saw a police car out there this morning. I'll meet you at her house.

Sarah grabbed her jacket and hurried up the street.

"You don't know Darius," Bernice was saying as she sat on her couch with her two friends, one on each side. "I know what you must think, but he has a good heart. When he came to me, he had just turned thirteen. His father was in prison, the courts had found his mother to be unfit, and he'd been in the system for several years. It was hard for him to make all those adjustments." She blotted her eyes on a napkin and continued.

"My husband was still living then, but he was already ill. He died the next year, and it was just Darius and me. It took a long time to win the boy over, but once he began to trust me, we became very close. At least I thought we were. He got into some trouble when he snuck out of the house, but he was always apologetic and always had an explanation. Maybe I wasn't firm enough...."

"What kind of trouble?" Sophie asked, but Bernice looked away, trying to avoid the question.

After a long pause, Bernice cleared her throat and attempted to answer, but her words seemed stilted. "It had to do with breaking and entering. I never quite understood the charges because I wasn't family. The child welfare department got all the details, and they shared what they wanted to with me. Drugs were involved, but Darius told me he didn't have anything to do with any of it. I believed him, but looking back now, he was probably lying. They put him in a juvenile facility for a while, but his lawyer got him out in a few months. The next time he wasn't charged. Maybe I was too lenient or too trusting. Maybe I shouldn't have been so quick to believe his explanations."

"Don't blame yourself, Bernice," Sarah responded. "He was raised in a terrible environment for the first eleven years of his life. It's almost impossible to make up for that kind of beginning."

"I know, but I tried. I loved the boy, but I couldn't really show it. He'd become agitated if I expressed any caring feelings for him. All I could do was offer him a safe home and consistency and hope that would be enough. I guess it wasn't ..."

"He was lucky to have you," Sarah said, trying to console her friend.

"It wasn't enough," she repeated.

Sarah put her arm around the woman and patted her gently.

The three women sat quietly for a few minutes when Sophie suddenly stood and announced, "We're getting all sappy again. Let's go cut fabric."

"I have an even better idea," Sarah announced. "Let's move over to my house and plan our presentation in detail."

Bernice smiled. "That's just what I need to get my mind off all this. What time shall we come?"

"You can come home with me now, or we can get together later."

Bernice thought for a moment, then responded, "I think I'll take a shower and rest for a while. I didn't get much sleep last night. How about 2:00?"

"Sounds fine," Sarah responded grabbing her jacket. "Sophie, I need to stop at your house and pick up Barney."

"I'll walk you across the street," Sophie responded as she grabbed her sweater.

"And I'll drive us to Sarah's later," Bernice said to Sophie, "thanks to your friend's generosity and that beautiful Volvo in my driveway."

On the walk home, Sarah thought about Bernice and tried to understand what she might be feeling. She knew Bernice had taken her responsibilities to the boy very seriously and cared deeply for him, at least for the person she had hoped he could become. Sarah wondered how she would feel in the same situation.

* * * * *

"Sophie and Bernice just drove up," Sarah called to her husband that afternoon.

"Do you need me for anything?" he called back from the computer room.

"No, I have us set up at the kitchen table, but I have coffee and cookies if you're interested."

"I'll come say hello," he responded once she mentioned the cookies. He suspected they'd be the good ones since she made them for her friends.

Charles wandered into the room once the women were settled, and his eyes immediately fell on the plate of cookies. He looked at his wife pleadingly.

"Help yourself, but they're not your fat-free ones, so don't overdo it," she responded to his implied question.

Bernice had looked much better when she arrived. Apparently, the rest had helped her. Sarah noticed that Bernice was watching Charles tentatively as if she were debating about saying something. Finally, she said, "Charles, I'd like to ask you a question. When that detective called me last night to say that my car had been found, I felt that there was something he wasn't telling me. He seemed to be choosing his words very carefully. I even asked him if there was more to it, but he just said that a detective would be getting back to me. Do you know anything more about this?"

Charles was taken aback by the question and found himself speechless at first, but managed to formulate a fumbling response. "Well," he began hesitantly, "I spoke with the lieutenant this morning … and the guy you talked to was right. They'll be sending a detective over to talk to you soon, perhaps tomorrow. I think that's a good question for you to ask him."

Seeming satisfied, Bernice simply replied, "Well, that's a relief."

That's a relief? Sarah asked herself. *He didn't answer her question.*

Charles was glad that she had accepted his response so easily, but his relief was short-lived. When he looked up at his wife, he saw that she was frowning and looking puzzled. *She knows that I just sidestepped the issue. She's going to be none too pleased with me when she learns the whole story.* Charles broke eye contact with his wife, took a deep breath, and said. "Okay, ladies, thanks for the cookies. I'm off to the computer room."

"What's he doing in there?" Sophie asked.

"I have no idea," she responded as she tried to set her suspicions aside. "He spends hours on that computer, and I try to stay out of it. It's usually some sort of police business. You know, he's still putting in a few hours a week for his old unit."

Bernice was starting to make notes and obviously unaware of the previous tension, but Sarah was aware that Sophie was staring at her inquisitively. Sarah shook her head almost imperceptibly and said, "Okay ladies, let's get our program on paper."

"I agree," Bernice responded. "We'll feel much better about it once we see it in black and white."

Sitting around the table, the three women began making final plans. They had previously decided on a short lecture about the history of feedsacks and how they were used during the first few decades of the twentieth century when fabric was scarce. "I'll tell a little about the history and display the feedsacks I'm keeping intact," Bernice said, "and Delores is going to loan me the items in her mother's trunk, so we'll have examples of some of the things women did with them. She has the two quilts we talked about using in my booth, a woman's dress, several children's items, dish towels, tablecloths, and lots of aprons."

"Let's spread them out on one of the tables," Sophie suggested, "and invite the participants to come up and look at them."

"Good idea," Bernice responded. "Also, I found several touching stories online that we could share. Would each of you be willing to tell one or two of the stories?"

"Sure," Sophie responded, looking mischievous, and Sarah knew she was already planning to be her colorful, flamboyant self. *Sophie loves an audience.*

"You could ask for audience participation at that point as well," Sarah suggested. "I'm sure many people will have memories to share." Smiling at Bernice, she added, "This is going to make an excellent presentation."

"I'll have lots of packets of pre-cut pieces for them to look at too."

"Or buy?" Sophie suggested.

"I don't know if you should sell them during the presentation or just refer them to your booth," Sarah responded.

"I like that better," Bernice said, looking excited. "This is going to be fun."

Charles walked through the kitchen on his way to the garage and caught Sarah's eye. He could sense her concern and felt like a heel for causing her distress.

I'll tell her what I know as soon as these women leave, no matter what Matt says. This isn't right.

* * * *

The two women had just left and were chatting excitedly about their plans for the presentation as they headed down the walkway to Bernice's loaner Volvo. "It looks like that went well," Charles said as he helped Sarah gathered up the coffee cups, leftover cookies, and various accouterments.

Sarah did not respond.

"I think I'd like to stop in at the quilt show and see the presentation in person."

Sarah did not respond.

Charles returned the cookies to the cookie jar, put the sugar bowl away, and turned to help Sarah load the cups and saucers into the dishwasher. She raised her head, looked him directly in the eye for the first time in the past few hours and firmly asked, "What's going on, Charles?"

Charles sighed. "I didn't want it to go this way, Sarah, and this afternoon I realized Matt was wrong."

"What does that mean?" she asked coolly.

"There has been a development, which Matt and the police department are not releasing to the public. He swore me to secrecy, and I agreed. I'm sorry now, and I realize that was wrong. I should have told you and trusted that you would not reveal it to anyone."

"Yes, you should have … at least the part about trusting me. Charles, if this is something you think should be kept between you and the police department, I will accept that." Her words were spoken more softly, but he could still see the hurt in her eyes.

Charles pulled out a chair at the table and asked her to sit. He had brought the morning paper with him and reached for it as he sat down across from her. "Did you read the paper today?"

"No, Bernice called early, and I rushed right over. What is it?

He laid the paper in front of her and pointed to the article on the front page. "Councilman Waterford's daughter was found murdered," she read aloud.

She unfolded the paper and looked at the picture of the lovely young girl. "Courtney," Sarah said as she read more of the article. "Only seventeen. Oh, Charles, this is terrible," she muttered. "I think there's a son too." She read on. "Yes, Steven. He's only thirteen. This is very sad."

Looking up at Charles she asked, "Do they know who did it?"

"That's what I wanted to talk to you about."

Sarah looked confused at first, but then her eyes grew wide open. "Wait. This is why you started acting so strange when Bernice asked you if there was something the police weren't telling her." Looking back at the paper, she added, "and this girl was found in Tennessee too. Charles, what's going on?" Sarah cried.

"She was found in the trunk of Bernice's car," he responded.

Sarah covered her mouth as if to stifle a scream. Tears welled up in her eyes. "Did they find Darius too?"

"No."

"But they are looking for him for her murder?"

"I think so."

"This will kill Bernice." She remained quiet for a few minutes, absorbing the whole thing. Then she added softly, "I see why you didn't tell me, Charles. I understand. I want to run right to Bernice, but I know I can't."

"You can when she knows," he responded. "The detective that's going to see her in the morning will be telling her. You might want to be there. In fact," Charles added, "maybe we should both be there."

"That's a good idea."

Charles stood and walked around the table to embrace his wife.

"I'm sorry I got so snippy with you, Charles. I should have trusted that you had a good reason."

"And I should have trusted you with the information. I guess we learned something today."

Chapter 9

"What are you folks doing on my doorstep at this early hour?" Bernice exclaimed cheerfully the next morning when she opened the door to find Sarah and Charles standing there. "I don't want to be rude, but that annoying officer is on his way over right now, so I can't invite you in, but if you go over to Sophie's, I'll be right over as soon as he leaves." Sarah saw that Bernice was still feeling the excitement generated the previous afternoon as they firmed up their plans for the show. It broke her heart to know what was in store for her new friend.

"We'd like to be here when the officer arrives, Bernice," Charles said in a solemn tone which she immediately detected.

"Have they found Darius?" she asked, her smile morphing into a worried frown.

"No," Charles replied simply, "but I think we need to be with you."

She nodded and stepped back, motioning for them to come in just as a police car pulled up in front of the house. Sarah saw that Sophie's curtains were drawn aside. She knew Sophie should be with them, but Charles had said they would include her as soon as the officer left.

"Detective," the officer said nodding his acknowledgment of Charles as he entered the house. The young officer had met Charles at the station the previous day.

"Good morning," Charles replied. "We are just here as friends, and my wife and I will wait in the kitchen while you talk to Mrs. Jenkins."

"No," Bernice exclaimed. "I want you two here. "What is it, officer?"

The officer was offered a seat but chose to stand, so Charles did as well but moved to the far side of the room. Sarah sat in a chair near him. "Mrs. Jenkins, you were told yesterday that your car had been located …"

"That's right," she responded with a question mark in her voice.

"What we weren't able to tell you at the time, and I'd suggest that you sit down for this," he added directing her to the couch. Bernice had a frightened look of anticipation on her face but followed his advice and sat.

"What didn't you tell me?" she asked.

"We weren't able to tell you at the time that there was a body found in the trunk." Charles cringed at the officer's lack of sensitivity.

The blood drained from Bernice's face, and she appeared to be about to faint. "Was it Darius?" she asked, grabbing her heart and looking pleadingly into the officer's eyes.

"No, no, sorry. It was a woman. …" the officer stuttered and looked to Charles for help. "I didn't mean …"

Sarah rushed to Bernice's side and wrapped her arms around her friend attempting to provide comfort.

"Does she need a doctor?" the officer asked apprehensively. "I can call for a bus."

Before Sarah could answer, Bernice said, "No. I'll be okay. Sarah, would you get my heart pills? They're on my night stand." Sarah nodded to Charles, and he headed for the bedroom that had been theirs.

When he returned with the pill bottle and a glass of water, Sarah was still holding Bernice in her arms, and the officer was nervously looking on. He later whispered to Charles that he hated delivering bad news to old folks. "You never know what it might do to them. ..." Charles, noting that the officer was young, tried to remember how he had felt in this sort of situation when he was new to the department. He hoped he had been more sensitive.

"I'm sorry," Bernice said, as she straightened up and Sarah was able to release her. "It was just such a shock, and I thought you meant …"

"I'm sorry, ma'am. There didn't seem to be any other way to say it, but I guess …"

"It's okay," Bernice responded. "About the body, was it the young woman whose picture was in the paper yesterday?"

"Yes," he responded. "Councilman Waterford's daughter."

"And the paper said she was murdered."

"Yes."

"Are you people thinking that my foster son Darius is responsible?"

"We have no suspects at this time."

"Are you looking for him?"

"Yes, he's a person of interest."

A person of interest, Charles repeated to himself. *They've already made up their minds that he did this. And maybe he did …?*

"Well," Bernice said, having pulled herself together. "I hope you find him, but for an entirely different reason. I want to see him cleared of this, and I want to know that he's okay. He did not kill this girl. He's been in plenty of trouble in the past, and I'll be the first to admit that, but I've never know him to hurt anyone. He was always a gentle boy. So find him, officer," she demanded as she stood and looked the officer in the eye with determination. "Find that boy and bring him home."

"We'll find him, ma'am."

How can she be so sure Darius wasn't involved, Sarah wondered, *considering all the surprises she's had to face about him lately? Does she really know him?*

"And when can I have my car back?" Bernice demanded, but immediately realized she didn't want the car back. "Never mind," she added, trying to keep her mind from imagining the body in the trunk. "Just keep it."

The officer left almost immediately after delivering the news, and he had no sooner pulled away from the curb that Sophie burst in the front door without knocking. "What's going on?"

As Sophie sat next to Bernice holding her hand, Charles and Sarah caught her up on what the detective had to say. Sophie had read the newspaper article when she got home the night before and had wondered if there was a connection. "Charles," she said, "You get to the bottom of this, okay?"

"Sophie, I'm not with the department anymore, and they've told me …"

"I know what they've told you, Charles. They told you to stay out of it, but I know that among the four of us, we can solve this. We've done it before," she added proudly, holding her head high. "Our friend needs our help."

"Let's go over to my house," Sophie announced. "I have a freshly baked peach cobbler in the warming oven and a pot of coffee brewing. "We need refueling so we can make our plans."

"Sophie," Charles began but was immediately interrupted by Sophie.

"Charles, you know we're going to do this with or without you."

Knowing she was right, he responded, "Okay, I'm in." *That way I can keep my eyes on these loose cannons.*

Once they were settled around Sophie's table, Sarah asked Bernice if she thought she'd feel like going to the quilt club meeting. "It's tonight, you know."

"I know, and I want to go. I promised to bring packets of feedsack squares to the meeting." With a look of confidence, she added, "And I intend to go on with my life. I know Darius didn't do this, and I know they'll find out who did. And if they don't," she added with a chuckle, "it sounds like we will."

Charles shook his head in disbelief. *Here we go again.*

* * * * *

Sitting across the desk from Lieutenant Stokely that afternoon, Charles listened to his friend's words while nodding compliantly. "I know, Matt. I know. I'm to stay out of the investigation, … I'm no longer with the department, … Detective Halifax is the lead detective and is totally in charge, … It's none of my concern, even if my friends are involved, … etcetera, etcetera. I know all that, Matt."

"So tell me this," Lieutenant Stokely responded. "Why is it you don't act like you know all that? Why are you in here asking me questions about the investigation?"

"I just want to make sure you're looking at all the possibilities," Charles responded.

Matthew Stokely sighed. *I wonder if I'll hang on like this once I retired?* He asked himself. "You've got to learn to enjoy your retirement, Charlie. Now I picture myself drifting around in the middle of a lake with my fishing rod and my beer chest."

Charles chuckled. "That sounds like a pipedream to me, Matt. I don't think you'll ever retire, even though I think you should."

"You're probably right," Matt replied, looking away and sighing. "You're probably right." Shaking off his momentary reverie, he turned to his friend and asked, "So what is it you think we might be missing?"

"What I've been thinking about is that this Waterford guy is in a contentious battle for the council seat in his district. Joe Capello is putting up a dirty fight.…"

"Hold it, Charlie. Surely you don't think Capello had anything to do with this. He may be a slimeball, but even he wouldn't kill a kid to win an election."

"Maybe not personally, but he has mob connections.…"

"Mob connections? Are you serious, Charlie? Those are unconfirmed rumors."

"They might be rumors out on the street, but I'll bet Major Crimes knows they are more than rumors. Have you talked to them, Matt?"

"Charlie, let it go. I've got work to do," he said as he stood, apparently dismissing his friend.

Charles stood and crossed the room to leave but hesitated with his hand on the doorknob. "Did this girl have a boyfriend?" he asked. "Have you checked into that?"

Lieutenant Stokely sighed and said, "Go home to your wife, Charlie."

Charles saw a flicker of sadness cross his friend's face.

Chapter 10

"Look at this, Sarah," Bernice commented as she gathered up the few packages of feedsack fabric that were left after the quilt club meeting. "The club bought at least half of the ones we cut." Bernice seemed surprisingly calm, even happy, and Sarah wondered what could have caused such a change in just a few hours.

"Save some for me," Ruth called from the stockroom. "My basket is almost empty." Ruth had bought a dozen or so packets to see how they would sell.

"We'll have to start cutting more right away," Sarah responded cheerfully. "The show is only two weeks away." Bernice just smiled as she tucked the checks into her purse and Sarah knew her friend was pleased. Bernice seemed to be coming to grips with what had happened over the past few days. "Darius is who he is," she had said on the drive over, "and I can't change that. I hope he didn't have anything to do with that girl's death, but if he did," she had added, "he will deserve whatever punishment is in store."

"Hey, girls," Sophie called across the room, pulling Sarah out of her reverie. "Delores wants to be on the stage with us when we do the presentation."

"That sounds great," Sarah replied, "especially since we'll be presenting her trunk load of items made from feedsacks." To Delores who was on her way over to the table where they were packing up, Sarah added, "I'm sure there'll be lots of questions about the items, and you'll be right there to answer them."

"I'm afraid I'll have to make up most of the answers," Delores chuckled. "My sister and I are the only ones left in the family who know anything about the old days."

"Why don't you bring your sister to the presentation?" Bernice suggested. "She can sit in the front row and be available if she knows an answer you don't."

"Good idea."

"I've been thinking about having Norman come too," Sophie announced.

"Hmm," Sarah responded. "He just might enjoy it. He's interested in the more creative side of life."

"That's true, but I thought he could be a plant."

"A plant?"

"If there's a lull, he can have a list of questions to ask to get things going."

"Not a bad idea," Sarah responded. "In fact, he might actually have some good questions since he'll probably be the only non-quilter in the room."

"So," Bernice began as she tucked the last of the fabric into her tote bag, "Are you ladies available to do some cutting tomorrow? I'll pay you with a good lunch and several pots of coffee."

"I'm in," Sophie responded enthusiastically.

"Me, too," Sarah said, "but I have an early morning appointment at the gym."

"The gym?" Bernice asked. "What's happening at the gym?" Sophie had given her a tour of the community center—the pool, the computer lab and classrooms, the resource center, and of course, the café, but hadn't taken the elevator to the bottom floor to see the gym.

"They've hired a trainer to work with people individually. I'm having an assessment in the morning and then she'll be setting up my program. She said it wouldn't take more than an hour."

"That sounds interesting. I'd like to …" Bernice began, but then she stopped talking, and Sarah knew she was still concerned about money. Although the credit card companies had put her accounts on hold during the investigation and weren't asking for payment, she was still worried about it. Sarah hesitated for a moment, looking for a way to address the financial issue tactfully.

"We're really lucky to have all these amenities in the village," she finally responded. "I understand there will be a small fee for the evaluation and plan, but the gym is available to everyone at no charge. Charles goes almost every day."

Bernice looked relieved. "I'd like to go with you in the morning and just walk on the treadmill while you meet with the trainer, if you don't mind," Bernice said. "That would invigorate me for my day at the cutting board."

"Great," Sarah responded enthusiastically. "I'll meet you there at 9:00."

As Sarah pulled into the garage, she could hear the phone ringing. "Sophie's on the phone," Charles called to her from the kitchen door. She pushed the button to close the garage door and hurried into the kitchen.

"Hi, Sophie. How did you get home before me?"

"Bernice thinks that new car is a race car," she joshed. "Anyway, I didn't have a chance to talk with you privately at the meeting, but I was dying to ask you something. What's up with Bernice?"

"What do you mean?"

"Well, she was a wreck just a few hours ago, and tonight she was acting like nothing had happened."

"She seemed almost relieved, didn't she? I noticed that too."

"Do you suppose she's heard from Darius?"

"Hmm. I hadn't thought of that, but it's a possibility, I guess." She was glad she didn't have the phone on speaker. This wasn't something she wanted Charles to hear.

Besides, it's just speculation, she told herself.

* * * * *

As Charles and Sarah were walking to the community center the next morning, he asked about Bernice.

"She's hanging in there," Sarah responded, already feeling guilty about withholding Sophie's theory from him. She knew Charles was referring to the murder, but she moved to the topic of the credit cards. "The credit card companies are doing the fraud investigations, and they've assured her they'll get to the bottom of it, so that's not worrying her too much. She's focused on her quilt show presentation. I'm just glad she has this to think about."

"She's a pretty strong lady," Charles said as he opened the door to the community center and stepped aside to let a man in a wheelchair go ahead of them.

"Have you picked out wallpaper yet?" Charles asked, pushing the elevator button that carried them to the lower level.

"I think so. I want you to take a look at it. ..."

"Sarah, I trust your judgment. What do I know about wallpaper?" he asked rhetorically.

"I'm worried about you hanging it alone," she began, but he cut her off immediately.

"First of all, I need the exercise, doctor's orders. And second, Jason has offered to help me when we're ready to do it."

"Jason?" Sarah exclaimed with surprise. "How nice. How did that happen?" Jason, Sarah's son, was always either working or involved with his family. His wife, Jennifer, had gone back to work, and they had agreed to share all the household responsibilities which were numerous with a toddler and an infant.

"We were talking about it at dinner last week, and he just offered. I tried to talk him out of it, but he was determined."

"I missed that. Where was I?"

"You and Martha had your heads together." Martha, Sarah's daughter, was settling into her new role as wife and mother, but still had many questions for her mother.

"Was Jennifer in on the conversation?" Sarah asked. "I'm surprised she can spare Jason."

"She was right there, and she encouraged him to do it," Charles responded. "When he went up to pay the bill, she whispered to me that she needs some alone time. She said you would understand," he added.

Sarah smiled, knowing that her son was somewhat of a control freak, and she was sure Jennifer could use a break from being told how to run the household. Her daughter-in-law had never complained to her about Jason, but Sarah knew him well enough to know he could be annoying in that department.

"When do you men plan to do this?"

"We need to work that out. I'll give you plenty of notice," he said, knowing his wife would want to secure all the furniture ahead of time.

Sarah, on the other hand, was making a mental note to arrange to be out of the house during the wallpaper project. She could imagine that it could become dicey as the two men, both with strong, in-charge-type personalities, worked out the details.

As she worked with the young trainer, Sarah glanced across the room where Bernice was walking on the treadmill and talking on her cellphone. Sarah saw her smile vanish and be replaced by a worried look. *Something has happened*, she told herself as she attempted to follow Tessa's instructions.

When Sarah arrived at Bernice's house later that morning, Sophie was already there. They had set up the kitchen for cutting the fabric and had brought piles of feedsacks into the room. Bernice didn't mention the call and Sarah didn't want to intrude, so she picked up a ruler, pulled her rotary cutter out of her pocket, spread the first feedsack out, and began to cut.

"I'm beginning to think I'll need another outlet once the show is over," Bernice was saying. "We've prepared several hundred packets, and we've barely made a dent in the second trunk.

"You might want to consider Anna's suggestion of selling through a website," Sophie remarked. "Or maybe on one of those consignment-type sites like eBay."

"Or," Sarah said thoughtfully, laying her cutting tools down, "perhaps you could sell them to quilt shops or place them in quilt shops on consignment."

"Interesting idea," Bernice said, also stopping and thinking about it. "I'll talk to Ruth about it. She might even be willing to put them on her website for a fee."

The three women were quiet for a while as they contemplated the possibilities.

"I may want to buy a few more packets myself, Bernice," Sarah announced as they were breaking for lunch.

"Really, I thought you had your quilt all figured out."

"I've decided to make a couple of throw pillows for the chairs in that room. Charles says they're uncomfortable."

"You think pillows will help?" Sophie asked, looking doubtful.

Sarah hesitated, then smiled mischievously. "No, but he doesn't know that, and they'll look cute."

Once they sat down to the lunch Bernice had prepared before the women arrived, Sarah could hold back no longer. "Bernice, I saw you on the phone earlier, and you looked worried. Is everything okay?"

Bernice sighed and laid her sandwich down. "I had my calls forwarded to my cell just in case. That was the credit card company that called."

"Oh?" Sarah responded, hoping the woman would continue.

"The two companies are working together on this now," she said, "and they wanted to know if I knew anyone in Central America."

"Why?"

"The man on the line told me that the charges on both cards were primarily made in Guatemala and Colombia.

"What? How did your cards get down there?" Sophie asked with surprise.

"They're working with the FBI now, but when I asked that question, the man said they were probably sold to a dealer down there."

"A dealer? A drug dealer?" Sophie asked.

"A dealer in stolen credit cards."

"Who would …?" Sophie started to say but glanced at Sarah who was almost imperceptibly shaking her head.

"Who would?" Bernice spoke up with anger in her voice. "I think we all know who would." Shaking her head and looking disheartened, she added, "About the time I start believing in that boy, he proves me wrong."

* * * * *

"They've stolen her identity," Sarah announced with anger in her voice. "Can you imagine that man doing such a thing to her? She was like a mother to him. …"

"Well, hon, this isn't exactly identity theft," Charles responded. "This is credit card fraud."

"What's the difference?" she demanded. "It still hurts her."

"Well, chances are the credit card company will get it worked out, so she doesn't get hurt too bad, if at all. Identity theft in its most serious form is when a person walks off with another person's identity. They become you. It's a much more serious crime and devastating for the victim. A victim of identity theft can lose everything and not even be able to prove who they are. The perpetrator walks off with their name, social security history, work history, pensions, even the title to their home sometimes … whatever they want. It can cost thousands and thousands of dollars in legal fees to get one's identity back, and it might not ever be resolved."

"Oh, Charles …" Sarah cried.

"Now, don't worry. This is credit card fraud. Your friend will come through this, perhaps a little less trusting, but she'll come through it."

"I hope you're right."

Sarah walked through the house and into her sewing room, where she sat and began stitching the remainder of her four-inch squares into four-patches. The gentle hum of her sewing machine always calmed her.

Chapter 11

Sophie and Norman had gone out for the day. There was a movie in town he wanted to see, and Sophie agreed to sit through a rough-and-tumble movie in exchange for a spicy meal at the new southwestern-style restaurant that had just opened in town. Sarah and Bernice were spending the day cutting and packaging feedsack fabrics, a task that was quickly becoming their full-time job.

Abruptly Bernice laid her rotary cutter aside, and Sarah could tell she had something on her mind. "What is it, Bernice?" she asked. "Has something happened?"

"No, it's not that," Bernice said reluctantly. "It's just that I have a rather embarrassing question for you."

Sarah set aside the bags she'd been filling with assorted six-inch squares and gave Bernice her full attention. "What is it?" she asked.

Bernice was quiet for a moment but then blurted out her question. "I met this man in the computer lab last week. He invited me to stop off in the coffee shop, and we talked for a while. He actually seems nice, and he wants to take me to dinner. I haven't been out with a man since my husband died, and I don't know what to do."

Sarah couldn't help chuckling with relief. "I think that's wonderful, Bernice."

"Do you? I don't know anything about him, but he said he's a good friend of yours and Sophie's, so I wanted to ask you what you thought."

"Who is this man?" Sarah asked, a bit baffled trying to figure out who she was talking about.

"His name is Andy."

Sarah laughed. "What a relief," she said, still chuckling. "You had me worried for a minute. Bernice, you couldn't have met a nicer man. He's been a friend of mine since I moved here, and Sophie knew him long before that. You can go out with Andy and be perfectly comfortable that you're in good hands."

"But he said he has a teenage daughter and at his age? I just don't know what that's all about."

"Bernice, Andy is an open and honest person. Just ask him to tell you the story about his daughter, Caitlyn. By the way, you already know her."

"I do?" Bernice frowned, trying to remember having met a Caitlyn.

"… from our quilt club," Sarah added.

"Caitlyn? Of course, I remember her now. She's an adorable young girl and seems very smart. That's Andy's daughter?" Bernice considered this new information for a moment, then asked, "What happened to his wife?"

"I'm going to let Andy tell you that story, but I can tell you that she died and Caitlyn came to live with her dad just a few years ago."

"The wife must have been much younger…." Bernice said as she contemplated this new information.

"She was, and there's a fascinating story that I'm sure Andy will share with you once you two get to know one another, but in the meantime, I can vouch for the man, and actually I think you'll enjoy going out with him. He's bright, energetic, fun, and always learning something new at the community center."

"I met him when I stopped by the computer center to see if there was anyone on the staff who could help me choose a new computer. Andy offered right away, and he doesn't even work there."

"No, but he knows all there is to know about computers, and he's very generous with his time. He's the one who got me into using the computer when I first moved here."

"So you think …?"

"Go to dinner. Give it a chance. I predict that you'll really enjoy spending time with him. And now, let's get these bags sealed up," Sarah added. "The quilt show is only three days away!"

Bernice sighed, then smiled, and began sealing bags.

* * * * *

"Bernice, we need to be on the road." Bernice came running out of the house, this time carrying another box of feedsack packets which she balanced on top of the others already loaded in the car.

"You never know," Bernice said breathlessly. "I don't want to run out."

"Remember," Sarah said, "Sophie and Norman have a box of assorted sizes in his trunk in case of an emergency. You have more than enough."

"And Delores is bringing her quilts for my booth?"

"She called me this morning from the road to tell me she had already left." They had planned to meet her at the security kiosk and caravan to Hamilton, but Delores said she had something to do and wanted to get to the show early. "So hop in the car," Sarah added patiently, "and let's get on the road."

It was just beginning to get light. The show was opening at 10:00 and they had planned to leave by 6:00 a.m. so they'd have several hours to set up. Ruth and her husband had gone the night before to get the Running Stitches booth set up, a much more complicated job than what Bernice was facing.

Once they were on the road, Bernice began to relax. "I think we have an excellent presentation," she said, going over the details in her mind.

"We do," Sarah responded. "Now, tell me about your date with Andy."

Bernice smiled. "We had a really nice time. We went to that new southwestern restaurant, La Bonita Café."

"And was it?"

"Was it what?" Bernice responded, looking confused.

"Cute. Doesn't *bonita* mean cute?"

Bernice chuckled. "Well, it was small and had intimate seating and flowers on the tables and curtains on the windows. Yes, I'd say it was cute," she added with a faint giggle which made Sarah smile.

"You had fun, I take it."

"I did. You are right about Andy. He's fun to be with and ever so kind and thoughtful."

"Did you ask about his wife?"

"No, in fact, I suggested we both leave our pasts for later. Actually, I didn't want to explain about Darius just yet. We just relaxed and had a good time."

Smiling, Sarah said, "I'm glad you decided to give it a try."

"Me too."

The two women drove in silence for a while when Bernice suddenly said she was desperate for a cup of coffee. "Do we have time to stop?" she asked.

"Sure," Sarah responded. "I'd like a bite to eat as well. I didn't have time to grab anything this morning." She pulled into a truck stop where she and Charles often stopped for coffee and the best pie in town. They took a table near the front and they both ordered coffee and a light breakfast.

"We haven't talked much about our elicit investigation," Bernice said after they had been served. "When do you think we'll get started?"

"I was hoping Charles would bring good news home from his contacts in the police department, but so far there's been no progress. Charles has been balking about us getting involved at all, but I figured we'd talk about it once the quilt show presentation was behind us."

Bernice responded excitedly. "I'm eager to get together to discuss a few ideas I've had."

"Such as?"

"Well, I think we've all agreed that the best way to clear Darius' name is to find out who killed the Waterford girl, right?"

"Right," Sarah agreed.

"So I've been wondering if the girl might have said something to her friends that could help us. She might have confided something that could turn out to be a lead of some sort," she added hesitantly. "I've never done anything like this before, but I was just thinking … or do you suppose the police have already checked that out?"

"Hmm. Interesting thought. I'll ask Charles if that's already been done. If not, maybe we could find out who they are and talk to them ourselves. That's a good idea, Bernice."

"But I don't know how we'd find out who her friends were. …"

"She was a senior in high school. Caitlyn might be able to help us," Sarah suggested. "They didn't go to the same school, but I know the schools get together for games and dances. They could have some mutual friends."

"Good idea," Bernice beamed.

For the next half hour, the two women sipped coffee and tossed around ideas about how they might learn more about the young girl's life. Suddenly, Bernice jumped up and cried, "The quilt show! We're late!" Both women left money on the table without waiting for the check and hurried out to the car.

Sarah headed up the road several miles an hour over the speed limit. "I think we're okay," she said as she pulled into the fast lane. "I don't believe that it'll take us long to set up the booth," and as it turned out, they had nothing to worry about.

The security guard who checked their passes directed them to Bernice's booth near the front door, and as they approached, they both stopped and gasped. "Delores!" Bernice cried. "It's fantastic!"

Delores, with a Cheshire cat grin on her face, was standing next to the booth, which she had decorated with a feedsack quilt spread across the table and another displayed in the middle of the large corkboard that provided a backdrop for the entire booth. Delores had then used corkboard hooks to hang items her grandmother had made using feedsacks: aprons, dish towels, a petticoat, a child's bloomers, an adult's dress, and a pieced tablecloth. In the center of the table sat a large rabbit made from feedsack fabrics in the design of a crazy quilt.

Delores had brought a dozen or so flat baskets for the table and had 3″ by 5″ note cards for labeling the sizes and prices. "You will have to fill out the cards," Delores called to the speechless Bernice. "And then you can slide them into these holders." She pointed to a pile of small plastic stands for the cards.

"Delores, I'm speechless," Bernice exclaimed. "This is fantastic. I never pictured it looking this professional."

"Let's take lots of pictures," Sarah said, pulling out her smartphone.

"Get some with customers too," Bernice added. She wasn't sure how she would do it, but she'd had so much fun with this project that she was hoping to find a way to continue it. It had brought excitement and creativity to her life.

Not long after the show opened, her booth was surrounded by customers asking questions about the feedsacks. The older women were reminiscing about the memories the fabrics were triggering. Instead of answering questions in detail, Sarah passed out flyers for the presentation and directed people to the sign-up table, encouraging everyone to come hear about them.

When Sophie and Norman arrived just before the presentation, Sarah sent Norman back out to the car to bring in the boxes of extra packets. "They're going pretty fast, and we haven't even had the presentation yet," she said.

It was nearly time for them to head over to the classroom when Bernice suddenly gasped. "We forgot something," she announced.

"What?" Sarah asked.

"We need someone to stay here at the booth during the presentation."

"But we're all on the stage," Sarah said.

"We could just close the booth I suppose," Bernice suggested, but Delores frowned.

"Security can be a problem at quilt shows," Delores said. "Not everyone here is a quilter, and our items are valuable, especially these vintage quilts and clothing. I'll stay behind."

"But we need you at the presentation," Bernice responded, "so you can explain how these fabrics were used."

"We've talked about this enough, Bernice. You and Sarah know all there is to know, and my sister will be in the front row. I'll tell her to take over for me."

Sarah and Bernice sighed almost in unison. "I guess that's what we'll have to do." Delores reached under the table skirt and pulled out the box of clothing she'd set aside for the presentation. Bernice carried the box, and the two women hurried to the classroom, both disappointed that Delores wouldn't be with them.

A few minutes later, Delores saw Norman heading toward the table. "Get over to the presentation," he announced as he reached the table somewhat breathlessly. "They're saving you a seat on the stage."

"I don't understand," she replied.

"I'm taking over here," he said. "Get moving. They need you."

Delores laughed and replied, "Well, I doubt that they really need me, but I'm glad I can be there. Thanks for doing this, Norman." She spent a few seconds emphasizing the importance of keeping the booth secure, but he had apparently been briefed already.

"I've heard some of the horror stories about quilts being lifted from shows, and I've seen the same thing in my business. Rest assured that I'll guard the booth well. Now get over there. They've already started the presentation."

"… and that's the history," Bernice was saying about a half hour later. "And now I'd like to introduce Delores. She has provided all of these examples of items made in the early twentieth century using feedsacks."

Delores stood and spent another twenty minutes showing completed feedsack articles and referring participants to Bernice's booth to see more. "Feel free to come up and look more closely. Touching is okay here, but, as you know, not out in the quilt show."

Some of the women came up to get a closer look, while others chose the time to ask questions of Bernice. Several people had stories to tell about their own experience with feedsacks and were encouraged to share their stories with the group.

The presentation was such a success that the participants had to be rushed out to allow the next class to come in. "If anyone is interested," Bernice called out above the noise, "just follow us back to my booth. There's more clothing and quilts there to see and plenty of feedsack fabric in case you're interested in making something."

To their surprise, at least half the room followed them to the booth. Norman's eyes grew as large as saucers when he realized the approaching crowd was headed straight for him.

Chapter 12

"So the show is behind you," Charles was saying at breakfast. "What next?"

"I'm going to work on the feedsack quilt today. I have most of my four-patches done, and I'm going to try to get it put together before our next quilt club meeting. Christina and Kimberly are holding a space for me."

"Holding a space?" Charles repeated, not sure what that meant.

"In their long-arm quilting schedule," she clarified. "They are going to take my quilt next if I can get it to them by Tuesday." Sarah still hadn't told Charles about her conversation with Bernice, but she intended to talk with him later that day.

"I have a surprise for you," he said in an intriguing tone.

"You have?"

"Didn't you notice the guest room door was closed when you came in last night?"

She had noticed, and she had smelled the wallpaper paste, but she had chosen to let Charles have the joy of presenting his surprise. "The guest room?" she responded innocently.

"As tired as I was when I got home last night, I just had my mind on sleep."

"Come on back," he said. Once they were in the hall that accessed the bedrooms, he opened the door with a flair and a broad grin.

"Oh, Charles, you got the wallpaper up. It looks fantastic. Even better than I had imagined."

"I'm glad you're happy with it," her husband replied looking quite satisfied with himself.

"How did you get all this done in one day? I thought it would take much longer." She gave him a hug and was glad she hadn't mentioned the paste smell the night before.

"I had lots of help."

"*Lots* of help?" She knew Jason had offered, but she couldn't imagine that his help would ever be described as 'lots of help.' Her son tended to prefer supervisory roles.

"Well, you knew Jason was helping, right?"

"Yes, and I'm glad he did."

"Andy heard about it from someone, maybe Caitlyn." He went on to explain that Caitlyn had stopped by to pick up Barney. She was meeting Penny, Sophie's granddaughter, at the dog park. "I told her it was a secret, but I guess she thought it was okay to tell her dad. Anyway, Andy showed up in the early afternoon and was a great help. That man's a real dynamo."

"Well, you had quite a crew in here, and it looks fantastic. How about a celebratory dinner at the steak house tonight, my treat?"

"It would be my pleasure to accept your kind invitation, my dear lady," he responded with a deep bow. "Now I have a question for you."

"What's that?" she asked, still walking around admiring the room.

"What's going on with your new friend and Andy?"

* * * * *

When Bernice answered the phone, she was surprised to hear Charles' voice. Having seen the name 'Parker' on the display, she assumed it was Sarah.

"Charles," she responded with surprise. "What can I do for you?"

"I've been wondering about something," he began. "Why didn't your credit card companies contact you when these unusual charges started appearing on your bill? I was under the impression they keep an eye out for things like that."

"That's my fault, Charles," she responded. "I asked the investigator that very question, and he told me that they tried, but my telephone had been disconnected. I had neglected to notify them that I had moved. It just wasn't high on my priorities because I knew I didn't owe anything. I intended to let them know once I got settled, but it slipped my mind."

"They should have mailed something then."

"They said they did, but it never got forwarded here."

"Well, I guess that explains it," Charles responded reluctantly. "I'd like to think they try harder than that."

"One other thing," Bernice said. "The investigator told me that when they saw that a ticket to Central America had been charged to the card, they figured I was traveling, and that explained the charges being made down there."

"Someone charged a ticket to your card?" Charles responded with surprise. "I wonder if Detective Halifax knows that."

"He must. They've been working with the credit card companies," Bernice replied, "but should I call him about this?"

"I'll take care of it," Charles responded. "They probably have a different department investigating the credit card problem, and it's just possible that the right hand hasn't talked to the left one. I'll straighten it out. This just might be very useful information."

They hung up, and Charles immediately dialed Matt's private number. "I think I know where Darius is," he said when the lieutenant answered.

"Where?"

Charles told Matt about his phone call to Bernice and the fact that there was an airline ticket that had been charged to her account. "That's where you can find Darius Mitchell."

"Yeah, we know about that Charlie. We've been looking at the credit card charges. I've been in touch with Guatemala, but they were no help. We've confirmed that no one flew on that plane by the name of Darius Mitchell or even fitting his description. The ticket was purchased with fake ID and a fake passport in the name of Ralph Turner who turned out to be a ninety-eight-year-old man in a nursing home who can't prove who he is because someone has stolen his social security card and his benefits are being paid to a phantom person in Jamaica. It's a mess Charlie, but it doesn't get us any closer to the Waterford girl's killer."

"Have you given any thought to my suggestion about someone on the Capello campaign?" Charles asked.

"Have you given any thought to my suggestion that you stay out of this investigation?" Matt retorted angrily.

Charles frowned as he attempted to formulate a response that wasn't too disrespectful when abruptly Matt apologized. "Sorry, Charlie. I'm just a little on edge. The captain has been on me about this case because of the politics and all. But to answer your question, we've bounced the idea around, and we feel it's pretty unlikely. Waterford is a popular politician, but he's local. This is small time politics—nothing that would justify murder for hire or the mob."

"But," Charles began but was interrupted before he could finish.

"Come on, Charlie. You know it was the kid. Just leave the investigating to Halifax. Hal's a good man. He can handle it."

Charles hung up feeling discouraged and thinking that Matt just might be right about him staying out of the investigation. *Why is it I can't seem to act retired like everyone else?* As he thought back over the times he'd become involved, he realized in just about every case he was trying to help his wife who was looking out for a friend. *And that's exactly what's happening this time.*

* * * * *

By the time he got home, Charles had resolved to leave the Courtney Waterford–Darius Mitchell issue to the police department and young Detective Halifax.

As he walked into the house, he was surprised by the delicious aroma of one of his favorite meals, roast leg of lamb. "What's the occasion?" he asked Sarah as he kissed her cheek.

"Dinner guests," she responded with a warm smile.

"Oh, yes, I guess it slipped my mind," Charles replied with frown lines indicating he was struggling to remember.

Sarah laughed, "You didn't know about this," she responded. "It was very last minute."

Relieved that he wasn't losing it, he asked, "Who's coming?"

"Two couples," she answered with a mischievous grin. "Sophie with Norman and Bernice with Andy."

"Bernice and Andy! Ah, I finally get confirmation of my suspicions. What brought this on?"

Sarah told her about how Bernice and Andy had met and about Bernice's reluctance to go out with him. "They've had a couple of dates, and they've gone well. Sophie and I just thought it would be good for them to spend an evening with other couples, just to see how nice it can be."

"Matchmaking!" Charles responded. "Never a good idea."

"We didn't do the matching, Charles. They found each other. We're just facilitating."

"Match-facilitating," he responded. "Just as bad."

"There's something else I wanted to ask you," Sarah said as she dried her hands and slipped the rice pilaf into the warming oven with the roasted vegetables.

"And what would that be?" he asked, opening a bottle of Bordeaux and setting it aside to breathe.

"What would you think of me doing a little volunteer work?"

"I think that would be just fine. Whatever you want to do is always fine with me. What are you thinking of?"

"Oh, I've been thinking about taking a look at Joe Capello's campaign. I understand they're looking for volunteers."

"Capello?" Charles exclaimed. "That guy doesn't espouse anything you believe in, Sarah. Why would you want to do this?"

"Because I'm a good listener."

Charles thought about that for a minute and suddenly realized what she was saying. "You're thinking of spying on the guy? Sarah, I can't let you do that."

"Excuse me?" she bristled.

"Okay, sorry," he quickly responded, realizing what he had said. "Of course, you're free to do whatever you want, but this could be very dangerous. What if you discover he's guilty? That would place you in harm's way."

"Oh, I have no intentions of going in there and accusing the man of anything. I just thought I could nose around a little. Besides, I wouldn't be alone."

"You wouldn't?" he asked.

"Of course not. Sophie would be with me."

"Oh, what a relief," he responded, trying not to sound too sarcastic.

Fortunately, at that moment the doorbell rang.

* * * * *

"Alright folks. I'm going to break this barrier of silence and ask the twenty-four thousand dollar question," Andy announced just as Bernice returned from carrying the last plate to the kitchen and Sarah had served the coffee and strudel. "What's the big mystery? You folks seem to all know something I don't know and I'm just too nosy a guy to be left out. What's going on?"

Everyone sat silently for a moment, but all eyes turned to Bernice. "Okay," Bernice began. "I was going to talk to

Andy about Darius when we got home, but perhaps this is the better place. Who wants to start?"

"It's your story, Bernice," Sarah responded. "Don't you want to tell it?"

"Actually, no. I'm tired of talking about it, and I'd actually like to hear Charles' take on it. Would you mind, Charles?" she asked, turning to the man she was beginning to appreciate being in her life.

Charles sighed and nodded his agreement, but instead of speaking, he left the table for a minute, returning with a newspaper apparently folded to a particular story. He handed the paper to Andy and said, "Are you familiar with this story?"

Andy scanned the page and responded that he had read it but hadn't heard anything lately. "Did they find the guy that did it?" he asked, but before anyone could answer, he added, "and what does this have to do with you folks?"

Not waiting for Charles to respond, Bernice spoke up saying, "That was my car she was found in."

"*What!?*" Andy exclaimed. "Okay, details please. Charles?"

Charles proceeded to tell the story of what had occurred over the past month and summarized the police involvement. "They are searching for Darius as a person of interest," Charles continued.

"So who is this Darius anyway?" Andy asked.

Charles turned to Bernice and said, "Do you want to take this question?"

"Yes," she responded, turning to Andy. "It's time to tell you about Darius." She proceeded to give some background about fostering the young boy, glossed over his run-ins with the police, and finally shared the part about borrowing her car, cleaning out her checking account, and finally the credit card fiasco.

"And now a body was found in that car," Andy responded. "Doesn't that mean he's the primary suspect?"

"I'm afraid so. …" Charles responded, giving Bernice a sympathetic nod.

"But we're hoping the real killer will be found first. That would clear Darius," Sophie interjected.

"Good grief, Bernice. You've been through all this since you moved here? I'm sorry I didn't know. I could have been helping." Turning to Charles, he asked, "Are you folks looking for him?"

"We're not exactly looking for Darius," Sophie responded. "We're doing our own investigation into who actually killed the girl. …"

"Wait a minute, Sophie," Charles interjected. "That's what the police are doing and what they've told us *not* to do."

"But Charles," Sophie responded, "you said yourself that they don't seem to be working in that direction. They're just looking for Darius, and you know they're going to charge him with the murder. His prints are all over the car, he stole the car …"

"Just a minute," Bernice cut in protectively, "I loaned him the car."

"To drive to Tennessee?" Sophie asked rhetorically.

"No," she said lowering her eyes and tentatively adding, "I guess he stole the car."

"Well," Andy said and sat quietly for a moment, apparently digesting what he had been told. "Well," he repeated, and Bernice looked at him, wondering if this was too much for him to take in. She was becoming very fond of this soft-spoken, kind man, and she hoped this complication wasn't going to cause him to back away from their friendship.

"Well," he said for the third time but with conviction this time. "I guess this means we'll become a six-person investigative team and get to the bottom of this."

Charles struck his own forehead with the heel of his hand and said, "I give up. Lieutenant Stokely is going to have us all arrested for interfering with a police investigation, but let's do it."

Everyone at the table cheered and Charles reached for the wine bottle and began filling their glasses. "Let's drink to our last days of freedom."

Chapter 13

"So, where do we start?" Andy was asking a few days later as the six friends gathered around the table in the Parker's dining room. Charles had objected to having their meetings at their house since he'd promised his old lieutenant that he'd stay out of the investigation, but it turned out to be the most space available to them.

Sophie had brought a fresh supply of 3″ by 5″ cards and was ready to start making a card file with all the clues they came up with, a technique she learned from one of her favorite mystery writers. "I think we should start by identifying all the possible suspects," she announced.

"I think we should start by selecting our leader," Andy announced, "and I nominate Detective Charles Parker." Everyone clapped and nodded their heads.

"And I refuse to accept the nomination," Charles announced.

"Charles! You're the obvious choice since you're an experienced detective," Sophie responded. "I second the nomination," she announced.

"Sophie, no," Charles responded. "I've promised Lieutenant Stokely that I'd stay out of the investigation and

I can't go back on that. I'm just here as a sort of consultant …
and to keep this group of renegades out of trouble, if I can."

"Okay, Charles. I guess we can accept that as long as you
are with us. How about Sarah?"

Sarah looked at Charles and saw that he was frowning.
"Perhaps I should pass for the same reason since I'm
his wife. …"

Sophie sighed. "Andy, you know the criminal system
from the inside. How about you?"

Bernice looked at Andy with concern, wondering what
Sophie's comment meant, and Andy dropped his eyes
looking embarrassed. "Well, I suppose you're right …"
Andy had spent time in prison a few years back when
he accidentally caused the death of his twin brother.
Unfortunately, he had chosen to leave town instead of face
up to his involvement and received a short sentence in a
minimum security facility. He hadn't shared this part of
his life with Bernice and could understand her concern.
"I think I'll need to talk with Bernice before I make
any commitment."

"Sophie?" Bernice said. "How about you?"

"I can't do all this paperwork and lead the group as well,"
she huffed.

"Well, I guess that leaves me," Norman responded.
"I'd be happy to be a facilitator, but I think we all should
be involved in every step since the police would say that
we're interfering in an investigation and we need to share
responsibility equally."

"Okay, it's decided," Sophie announced. "Norman, the
floor is yours."

Norman cleared his throat and sat up straighter in his chair. "Well, as Andy said, I think we should start by identifying all the possible suspects."

"Councilman Capello with the help of his mob connections," Sarah called out.

"A boyfriend we don't know about yet," Sophie suggested.

"How about some random person they met on the road?" Andy suggested.

"Are we going to consider the possibility that Darius did it?" Charles asked, and everyone frowned at him.

"We're here to prove someone else did it," Bernice reminded him. "The police are already working on the theory that Darius did it."

"Sorry," Charles responded. He didn't want to admit it to this group, but he suspected that the police had it right.

"Anyone else?" Norman asked, looking at Sophie who was writing down the potential suspects.

"There could be lots of other people, but we don't know who they might be. Bernice mentioned the other day that perhaps we could find a way to talk with the young girl's friends," Sarah said.

"My daughter, Caitlyn, said she knows at least one of Courtney's friends," Andy offered.

"We should talk to that friend, and we might get the names of some others from her," Bernice responded.

"I'd be happy to do that," Andy offered, "Caitlyn could even help me get to these other kids."

"Maybe you can find out about boyfriends at the same time," Bernice added.

"Hold it," Sophie called out. "I need to start a file on suspects and another one on who's doing what."

"I'll freshen our coffee cups while you catch up," Sarah said, standing and heading for the kitchen.

When she returned with the coffee pot a few minutes later, Charles was saying, "Although I'm not an official part of this investigation, I'm the only one with access to the law enforcement computers. How about I do a search for similar crimes in the area. That might follow-up on Andy's 'random person' theory." *Darn. Didn't I just say I was keeping out of this?*

"Great idea," Norman responded.

"One other thing I've been thinking about," Sarah began thoughtfully. "How did this girl end up in Bernice's car? Where did she meet Darius? How can we find out about that?"

The group was quiet as they mulled over her question. Finally, Andy spoke up saying, "Maybe that answer will come from one of her friends. I'll try to find out where she might have wanted Darius to take her, or if she was in the habit of taking off with strangers."

"You might even learn that there were places she liked to hang out," Bernice suggested. "She could have met him at a bar. I know she was too young to drink, but from that picture in the paper, she looked older than she was."

"Good point," Andy said, smiling at her. He was pleased when she smiled back reassuringly. He hoped she would understand about his past when he talked to her later. They had a dinner date, and he hoped she wasn't going to cancel it now that she knew about his prison record.

"Well," Norman began. "It looks like we have a few assignments. Andy will be pursuing the friend angle, Charles will do some computer searches. Bernice, would you think about anything Darius has said to you that could lead to where he might have been going? Why was the car found in Tennessee? And, let's see …"

"I'll get these cards filed in order and type up notes about today's meeting," Sophie offered. Sarah smiled, realizing that her friend was taking this recording responsibility way too far, but, as Charles said, it keeps her out of trouble.

"Sarah, what would you like to do?"

"I've had an idea, but Charles is giving me grief about it. I'll talk to him again and tell you the next time we meet." Sarah felt that she could get a feel for any possible connection Joe Capello might have with the murder if she could get into campaign headquarters as a trusted volunteer, but Charles vehemently objected.

"By the way, when will we get together again?"

"How about this weekend, perhaps Saturday night?" Norman suggested, "and I'd like for you to come to my new place in town. In fact," he added, "I'll even provide dinner."

* * * * *

Sophie, Sarah, and Bernice were sitting in Sarah's sewing room. Charles had gone to the gym, and the rest of the group had left. "I think we got off to a good start," Bernice was saying. Sarah looked at Sophie and raised an eyebrow. Sophie knew she was asking if now was the time to confront their new friend. They had discussed it at length on the phone that morning and decided it had to be done. Sarah had suggested that they wait until after the meeting in case

Bernice was planning to let everyone know while they were all together. But she hadn't.

"Bernice," Sarah began. "Sophie and I have a question we need to ask you."

"Okay," Bernice responded with a relaxed smile. "Anything. What's up?"

"We hope you won't be upset with us for asking, but we've been confused by the sudden change in your demeanor about Darius and the body found in your car."

"What do you mean?" Bernice asked with a confused frown.

"The day the detective told you about the body we were all together. You were absolutely devastated, and rightly so, but that same evening you were all bright and cheerful. Did you speak with Darius?"

"What? Why would you think that? If I had talked to him, wouldn't I have told you?" she responded somewhat indignantly as she stood and walked toward the door.

She didn't really answer the question, Sarah realized, and she wondered if Sophie noticed it too.

Sarah didn't have to wonder for long. "Bernice, answer the question," Sophie demanded. "Have you spoken with Darius since he disappeared with your car?"

Bernice was silent.

"Okay," she finally said, returning to the futon where she had been sitting with Sophie. Resting her elbows on her knees, she dropped in head into her hands and sighed.

"Bernice?"

"I should have told you both about this, but he said not to tell anyone."

"You've talked to him, then?" Sophie asked, sounding impatient.

"No, not actually, but the same day that the officer told me about the body, Darius left a message on my machine. He said he wanted me to know that he had nothing to do with the girl's death, but that he needed to stay out of sight until the police found the real killer. He said that with his record, they would charge him without looking for anyone else. He was scared, and he just wanted me to know that he was okay." Bernice began to sob. "I should have told you, but …"

"We understand," Sarah said reassuringly.

"Speak for yourself," Sophie said. "This changes everything."

"What does it change?" Bernice asked, wiping her eyes.

"Well, now we know he didn't kill the girl."

"No, we don't know that, Sophie," Bernice replied much to Sarah's surprise. "All we know is that he's alive. I've come to grips with the reality that Darius lies to me, but I also know that he is a caring person. He cared enough to know how worried I'd be and he let me know he's okay. And if he did this terrible thing, then he'll have to pay the price. I'm just relieved to know he's alive. I was afraid that whoever killed the girl might have killed him too."

"You know, Bernice, we need to tell this to the group. And I will have to tell Charles."

"I know. I almost told everyone at our meeting, and I'm sorry I didn't."

Sophie and Bernice were climbing into Sophie's car when they saw Charles jogging toward the house. Charles noticed that Bernice was avoiding eye contact and was looking worried when he walked over to say hello.

"What's with Bernice?" he asked a few minutes later as he came through the kitchen door.

"There's been a development," his wife answered as she handed him a bottle of spring water.

Chapter 14

"Good morning," Sarah said as she sat down to talk with Andy who had just called. After a few minutes of friendly chatting, she asked, "Are you looking for Charles?"

"Actually, I'm looking for you this time."

"Oh?"

"I want to ask you a big favor. I talked with Caitlyn last night about Courtney. Unfortunately, she didn't know the girl personally. She said they were at the same party a couple of times, but she never had an opportunity to talk to her, but she told me a few interesting things."

"Tell me," Sarah prompted.

"For one thing, this Courtney girl was very tight with an older boy. His name is Douglas, and he's in his second year at the university. She said they were always together at least at these parties, and she left with him both times."

"Did you get his last name?"

"Caitlyn didn't know any more about him, but she told me about this girl, Amber Nash, who was Courtney's best friend."

"Excellent. How can I help?"

"I don't think Amber's mother would be especially happy to get a call from a strange man asking permission to meet with her daughter."

"Hmm. You're probably right. Do you want me to call her?"

"More than that," Andy replied hesitantly. "I was hoping you'd go with me to interview the girl. If you could set it up, we could meet with Amber and her mother."

"Amber might be more forthcoming without her mother present, but I'll see what I can do. When do you want to do this?"

"Whatever you can arrange will work for me."

As Andy was giving Sarah the Nash's phone number, Charles strolled into the kitchen, and Sarah mouthed that Andy was on the phone. She lifted an eyebrow questioningly and pointed toward the phone nonverbally asking if he wanted to talk to him. She knew he'd been wanted to meet Andy for a game of racquetball. Charles nodded, and Sarah signed off saying, "I'll let you know what I find out. Charles wants to speak to you," and she handed the phone to her husband.

After they had breakfast, Sarah placed a call to Amber's mother and explained the situation. Mrs. Nash was reluctant at first but ultimately agreed to allow her daughter to meet with them as long as she could be present. They arranged to get together the same afternoon. Sarah sighed as she hung up, hoping the daughter would be entirely truthful with her mother there.

As it turned out, she had nothing to worry about. Amber was eager to do anything she could to find out what had happened to her friend. She was, however, very protective of her friend's reputation and primarily helped by giving Andy and Sarah the names and phone numbers of some friends who she said would have more information. Sarah noticed that Amber chose her words very carefully when asked questions about Courtney's behavior at these parties. *She doesn't want to talk in front of her mother*, Sarah realized. She wondered if they might be able to get into one of these parties to question the kids alone.

Amber knew the young man Courtney had been seeing, and she made it very clear that she didn't approve. "His name is Douglas Kester. We knew him back in junior high," she offered. "He was a few years ahead of us and really wild. I tried to talk her out of dating him, but she felt lucky that a college boy was interested in her."

Suddenly, her eyes grew very wide. "Do you think he had anything to do with Courtney's murder?" she asked, looking from Sarah to her mother and back to Sarah with a fearful look on her face.

"Do *you* think he did?" Andy asked. Andy had left most of the questions to Sarah but felt compelled to pursue this himself.

Amber was quiet. "I don't know," she finally responded thoughtfully. "I didn't like him, but … I don't know. Are you going to be talking to Doug?"

Doug? Sarah thought, wondering just how well Amber knew the boy.

Once they got into Andy's car, he handed Sarah the list of phone numbers. "Hang on to these, will you? You'll probably be making the calls anyway if you don't mind."

"Are we going to talk to Douglas? And did you notice she called him 'Doug' when she wondered if he could have killed Courtney?"

"I noticed that, but it doesn't necessarily mean anything. I'm sure Courtney called him Doug when she talked about him to Amber."

"And are we going to talk to him?" she asked again.

"Let's see what we get from the others. This might be a better interview for Charles to do, assuming he's willing to. I know he wants to stay on the sidelines."

As they drove past the Cunningham Village kiosk, Sarah said, "Drop me off at Sophie's, if you don't mind. I want to tell her about the interview and get all these names and numbers into her fancy recording system."

Andy chuckled. "It's a rather extravagant system, but it just might turn out to be useful."

"Charles says it keeps her busy and out of trouble. I love my friend, but she can be rather impulsive. She'd be on her way right now to the Kester house demanding to know if Douglas killed the Waterford girl."

They both laughed, and neither was surprised when Sophie came rushing out of her house as they pulled up. "What happened? Did you find out who killed the girl?" she asked excitedly.

* * * * *

Sarah spent the afternoon in her sewing room. She had partially finished three projects and was beginning to feel scattered. "I'm going to finish off the feedsack quilt first," she told herself aloud, "and get it to the quilter."

She then picked up her embroidery hoop wall hanging and put it into a plastic project box along with a few spools of thread in compatible colors. The wall hanging involved hand piecing hexagons together randomly until the piece was large enough to snap into an embroidery hoop.

"This I can work on at quilt club meetings or sitting in the living room with Charles in the evenings," she said to herself.

"Are you talking to me?" she heard her husband call out from the computer room.

"No, dear. I'm just getting organized."

The only other projects she had started were the pillows that she was making for the guest room. She had purchased two scrap bags of feedsack fabrics from Bernice and was going to sew them together in a crazy-quilt style, but she hadn't worked out the details yet, so she put that project in another box and set it aside for now.

"So you're all organized now?" Charles called to her as she passed by the computer room door.

"I have the guest room projects organized, but once that's done, I have several UFOs in the cabinet that I want to get back to."

"Unfinished Objects!" Charles announced proudly. "See, I listen." Sarah chuckled as she continued up the hall toward the kitchen.

"Come on, Barney. Let's go pull some weeds." Barney came running, responding excitedly to his favorite word—'Go.'

* * * * *

Charles was again sitting across the desk from his friend and ex-superior, Lieutenant Matt Stokely. Matt's desk was covered with file folders, and he was making notes on a yellow legal pad. Charles waited quietly until Matt indicated he was ready to listen. Finally, the lieutenant laid his pen down, sighed, and looked directly at Charles.

"So what is it now, Charlie?"

There weren't many people left at the station that still called him Charlie. Most of his cohorts had retired long ago. Matt still hung in despite departmental encouragement that he retire.

"It can't have anything to do with the Waterford case, I'm sure," Stokely continued, "since you assured me you aren't going to get involved with that in any way."

Charles shrugged, feeling sorry that he wasn't able to tell Matt about his friend's efforts. At least he wasn't personally involved. *At least not much.*

"I do have something to tell you about that case, but it's not because I'm involved. It's because Sarah is friends with Darius' foster mother and she shared something with Sarah that I think you need to know."

"Okay," Matt responded with a deep sigh of resignation. "What is it?" He looked tired, and Charles wondered if he was sleeping. The sparkle he had always had in his eyes had long since faded.

"She got a call from Darius," Charles said, wishing he had better news to give his friend.

"What?" Matt thundered. "The foster mother?"

"Yes," Charles replied.

"Does Halifax know this?"

"Not that I am aware," Charles responded, glad that his answer confirmed his lack of involvement in the case.

"*Not that you know of?*" Stokely shouted. "Didn't you ask?"

"That might have been construed as 'interfering in the investigation,'" Charles responded calmly, trying not to let the sarcasm in his voice be too obvious.

Lieutenant Stokely's face was beet red as he picked up the phone and demanded, "Get Halifax in here right now."

Charles watched as his friend pulled an almost empty pint from his desk drawer and added the remainder to his coffee. He remembered another officer who had done the same, leading to the end of his career. "It's time for you to retire, Matt," Charles said in a gentle tone.

"I know," his friend muttered as he pushed the mug aside. "But there doesn't seem to be much reason now that Doris is gone."

The two men remained silent, Charles because he didn't know what to say, and Matt because he never talked about the sudden and tragic death of his wife the previous year.

Detective Halifax tapped on the door and stuck his head in saying, "You wanted to see me, Lieutenant?"

"Have a seat," Matt responded, sounding somewhat more in control.

"Lieutenant," Halifax said once Matt explained about the phone call, "there's no way I could have forced that information out of the woman if she didn't volunteer it. She's not a suspect. She never let on in any way that the guy had contacted her. In fact," he added, "I asked her more than once."

"Well, we can sure interrogate her now," he responded. "She lied to an officer and withheld information in a murder investigation. Those are crimes in any state."

"Do you really want to go after this woman?" Charles asked, momentarily stepping out of his bogus role as an uninvolved bystander.

"I guess not," Stokely responded resting his elbows on the table and burying his face in his hands. "I just wish we had something—anything. The Chief is on my back about this. He wants it solved now. He's got the governor on his back. I hate politics," he muttered as he stood and nodded toward the door, apparently dismissing the two men.

As he drove home, Charles reflected on the years he had worked for the department and, for the first time, acknowledged that his stroke and subsequent retirement had been a lucky thing. *I'd be dead by now*, he told himself, contemplating the effect that continued stress would have had on his body.

Charles vowed to have a serious talk with Matt about retiring. He remembered a time when Matt was full of energy and life—*a good-natured man, fun to be around*. Charles reflected on those years and had to admit that every good time he could remember with Matt involved Doris as well.

The Stokelys had never had children, and when he lost his wife to a drunk driver, he threw himself into his work. He'd been eligible to retire for the last couple of years but hung in, probably because it was the only life he had any more. *And now the political pressure*, Charles mused.

Charles vowed to stay on his friend about retiring. They could find things to do together. "Who knows?" he said to himself. "Maybe I could sit in that row boat in the middle of the lake with my friend, at least once in a while. It doesn't sound all that bad. A little boring maybe, but not bad."

Chapter 15

The next meeting of the "Undercover Sleuth," as Sophie was now calling their rogue investigative team, was much livelier than their first one. The group spent the first half hour touring Norman's luxurious condominium in the Barkley House, a new high-end building on the north side of town overlooking the lake. His unit was on the nineteenth floor which was, in fact, the top level but he discouraged his friends from calling it the penthouse. "Too pretentious," he had said. Two sides of the living room were windowed, floor to ceiling and overlooked a wraparound balcony lavishly decorated with greenery. "Most of that will come inside this winter," Norman commented.

Sarah had never noticed how humble Norman was, side-stepping and downplaying all compliments. "He's quite a catch," she whispered to her friend Sophie with a wink. "He's done very well for himself."

"Oh, stop," Sophie responded with a dismissive hand gesture. "You know I don't care about that kind of stuff."

"Well, at least he's comfortable," Sarah added.

"Who wouldn't be in this place," Sophie responded, looking around for the dining room. "Where do we eat?"

"Right this way," Norman called right on cue, directing his guests into the dining room. The table was not only large enough for the six of them, but another dozen or so would have been able to join them. Pushing a button, he remotely opened the curtains exposing another view of the lake and the waterfront park.

Norman had just finished pouring wine and making a toast to their sleuthing success, as he put it, when two serving people entered the room. Each guest was served a delectable meal consisting of a Cornish hen, mushroom dressing, and asparagus with hollandaise sauce. The meal was followed by coffee and a scrumptious, artery-clogging dessert, which caused Charles to swoon as he lifted each bite to his mouth.

"Do you suppose he had this meal catered?" Sophie asked Sarah when they were alone later in the evening, and Sarah responded that if Norman cooked the meal himself, she must marry him immediately.

They took their wine glasses and settled down comfortably in the living room for their meeting. Andy and Sarah had the most to report. After talking about their meeting with Amber, Andy explained that the girl had given them a list of some of Courtney's other friends. Sarah had contacted the parents and, with the exception of one family, had received permission to talk with the teens at a local coffee shop where the group got together on Friday nights. All of the parents were concerned about what had happened to Courtney and seemed pleased that someone was looking into it besides the police. One father, himself a private detective, had said, "When politics are involved, an investigation can really get fouled up."

Sarah and Andy went on to report that on the previous Friday night they had met Amber and her mother at the coffee shop and Amber had introduced them to Courtney's friends. To Sarah's surprise, they seemed eager to talk about Courtney and particularly her rather wild habits.

"She was just asking for trouble," one of the boys had said shaking his head soberly. Although no one in the group confessed to drinking themselves, they pointed out that Courtney frequented a bar on the west side of town and, before she met Douglas, had a reputation for picking up older men.

"Did her parents know?" Sarah had asked.

"According to Courtney, they didn't care," one girl volunteered.

"I'm not sure I believe that," Amber had added. "I've known Courtney since sixth grade and her mother always seemed to care about her. I think they had a pretty good relationship, but her father wasn't around much."

"I wonder if we should talk to Courtney's parents," Norman speculated.

Charles responded, shaking his head and saying, "Absolutely not. That would definitely be interfering with the investigation, Norman. No way can we go near her parents."

"I guess you're right," Norman replied, "but I feel as if we're missing a vital piece of information."

Andy went on to explain that he had visited the bar the previous night. "The bartender said that the last time he saw her, she was leaving with a scraggly looking guy in his early twenties."

"The description sounds like Darius," Sarah said.

"I went back this morning and showed him the picture," Andy added. "It was Darius."

"I don't guess there was really any question in our minds that she left with Darius since she was found in my car," Bernice said.

"Not necessarily," Charles interjected. "Someone else could have stolen the car and taken Courtney."

They went on to discuss the possibility that Douglas, the current boyfriend, might have played some part. Charles reported that he'd done a computer search of the law enforcement databases and couldn't find anything on him. "Of course, that can just mean he hasn't been caught. He's skirting the law just by going out with an underage girl."

"Were you able to find out why they might have been driving to Tennessee?"

"Amber spoke up and said that Courtney was just leading Douglas on," Sarah responded. "She had this guy down in Tennessee that she met online. She told her friends they were in love, but actually, they'd never met. She wanted to go to Tennessee and surprise him according to Amber. Andy and I suspect that's where Darius was taking her."

"It would be like him to do that," Bernice added. "Sure, he made a lot of bad decisions, and this was probably one of them, but he was always ready to help people when they were in trouble. He understood having trouble …"

"Charles, do you have anything to tell us?"

"I haven't found anything helpful on the department's computers. Detective Halifax is still assigned to the case, but they haven't entered any updates on the investigation. Due to the politics involved, they're playing their cards close to the vest. I also scanned for similar crimes between here and where the car was found," he continued. "There were a few carjackings, and I realized that could be a possibility. Of course, they could have picked up a hitch-hiker who turned on them. There was a jailbreak in southern Kentucky at about that time, and it's conceivable that they picked up a couple of convicts on the run, but I think that's pretty unlikely."

"That's a scary thought," Sophie commented as she grabbed another card and entered it.

"The two guys took off from a minimum security facility, both there on drug charges, and I didn't see any reference to them being dangerous. My gut tells me that's not the route to follow."

"Bernice?" Norman began. "Have you thought of anything that might help us?"

Bernice became flushed and dropped her eyes for a moment, but then raised her head and said, "I have a confession to make. I should have told you folks at our last meeting, but I've told Sarah, and now I want to tell everyone." She proceeded to describe the message on her machine from Darius and attempted to explain why she had kept it to herself. "I should have told the detectives. I guess I was still somewhat under his spell. He asked me not to tell, and I didn't."

"I told Lieutenant Stokely and Detective Halifax earlier this week," Charles offered. "Of course, he wished they'd known earlier because they might have been able to trace the call, but they understand and are moving on. Thanks for telling everyone tonight, Bernice. I know that was hard."

"I'm just so ashamed of how I've allowed myself to be taken in by this young man," Bernice said apologetically.

"You raised the boy, Bernice," Sarah responded. "You're the only family he knows, and he's like a son to you. I think it's admirable that you have stuck by him and trusted him over the years."

"I agree," Andy chimed in while the others nodded in agreement.

"The positive thing we can take from this information is that we know now that Darius is alive," Sarah added.

"Good point, Sarah. So, does anyone have anything else?" Norman asked.

"One other thing," Charles added. "I told Sarah that I'd be willing to interview the boyfriend, Douglas Kessler. He might have reason to go after her considering she dumped him for what she thought was a quicker way to get to Tennessee."

"Good idea, Charles. Just don't get yourself in trouble with the lieutenant," Norman commented.

"If there's nothing else …" Norman began, but Charles again spoke up.

"There's still that Capello issue. I've tried unsuccessfully to get the department interested in looking at the political aspect of this."

"You think Capello could be involved?" Andy asked. "Do you think he'd go to such lengths just to win a local election? I mean, we're talking about murder here."

"Maybe it was intended to be a kidnapping just to distract Waterford long enough for Capello to make some headway with the voters," Charles suggested.

"I don't know how we could look into that. …" Norman pondered.

"I've already come up with how to deal with that one," Sarah interjected, "but I've been shot down."

"How's that?" Bernice asked.

"I suggested that Sophie and I volunteer to help at their campaign headquarters. We could keep our ears open and find out what's happening on the inside. Charles says it's too dangerous."

"I agree completely, Sarah. If they'd do something like this, they're too dangerous for you to be around," Norman responded.

"I agree, too," Andy added. "That's too dangerous for you two."

"The big brave men looking out for the little ladies?" Sarah mumbled looking irritated, and Sophie chuckled.

"Sarah," Charles began, not wanting to continue their argument in public, but wanting the others to understand his point of view, "Capello is known to have mob connections. You're talking about getting close to some dangerous folks." Sarah didn't respond, but he could see that the others agreed with him. "How about I keep working on the department to follow up on this. They are the ones that should be doing this kind of investigation."

For someone who doesn't want to get involved, Sarah thought, *my husband sure stays in the thick of it.*

"If you're willing to do that, Charles, I think that's the answer," Norman said.

Everyone except Sarah nodded their agreement, including Sophie.

"Well, if that's it, I guess we're finished for tonight. Let's all go home and see if we can think of anything else we can do."

As the meeting was breaking up, Norman's guests showered him with praise for both the food and the accommodations. As Sarah watched him responding to the praise, she noticed how humbly he accepted the compliments. She was glad Sophie had him in her life.

Driving home, Charles reached for Sarah's hand, and she moved closer to him. "Sorry, hon," he said without explanation. She knew what he meant.

"It's okay. You're probably right." A few minutes later, she commented, "That was a lovely evening, wasn't it?"

"The cause that brought us all together is rather morbid," he responded, "but our friends are some of the nicest people I've ever known. Every one of them is kind and caring."

"And they'd do anything for any one of us. I feel very fortunate to be where I am at this point in my life."

"It wasn't just by chance, sweetie. You've made a good life for yourself. I see men and women around the village that seem to be just waiting to die. They focus on their ailments instead of what's good about their lives. As far as I'm concerned, life is meant to be lived with gusto right up to the end."

Sarah chuckled and squeezed his hand.

Chapter 16

"Charlie, sorry to call so early in the morning, but I knew you'd want to know." Charles was groggy when he answered the phone and didn't immediately recognized the voice. He glanced at the display and saw it was Detective Halifax and at the clock and saw that it was 4:30 in the morning.

"That's okay, Hal. What's up?" He responded as he held back a yawn.

"It's Matt, Charlie. He had a heart attack on his way home last night and is in intensive care."

"How serious?" Charles asked as he threw the covers back and stood up.

"Serious, Charlie. Very serious. He spent the night in surgery, and the doc says it's touch and go at this point. No one's allowed to see him. The Chief wanted me to call you to see if you know about any next of kin. Records only show the wife, and of course, she's gone now."

"He's never mentioned anyone," Charles said, still feeling the effects of the shock. "You say it's very serious?"

"Yeah, Charlie. You might want to come over to the hospital. You're closer to him than anyone."

Sarah turned on the light and gasped when she saw her husband's face. "Charles, what is it?"

He gestured that he would tell her in a moment. His face was ashen, and she could detect a complex combination of emotions—worry, fear, even anger. She knew immediately that the call wasn't family—he would have told her right away. She thought she had heard him say "Hal." *It must have to do with the Department.*

When Charles hung up the phone, he collapsed on the side of the bed looking defeated. "It's Matt," he finally said. "It's his heart." He told Sarah what little he knew. "Hal said he was driving home when the pains started. He ended up in the hospital with open-heart surgery."

"I heard you say that it's serious. Will he be okay?"

"That's all I know. They want me at the hospital."

Sarah pulled on her robe and slippers and headed for the kitchen. "I'll make you a quick breakfast while you shower. Do you want me to go with you?"

"I'll probably be just hanging around there most of the day. I'll call and let you know what's going on." As he headed for the bathroom, he realized Sarah had come back into the bedroom looking worried.

"Charles, what happened about that test Dr. Grossman was scheduling for you?"

"Oh no," he responded as he hit his head with the heel of his hand. "I totally forgot about that. His nurse called me a couple of weeks ago to set it up, and I told her I'd call her back."

"Charles …"

"I know, hon. I'll call the office today once I know what's going on with Matt."

"I hate to say this, Charles, but that could be you in that hospital. It scares me to think what could happen."

He reached over and pulled her into his arms. "I know, and I'm sorry. I just got wrapped up in this case. I'll take care of it today, I promise."

* * * * *

When Charles pulled into visitor parking, he saw eight or ten officers from the Department leaving. *Not a good sign*, he thought, but then realized it could, in fact, be an excellent sign. "Maybe things are looking up," he told himself hopefully.

He bypassed the reception area, flashing his outdated Department ID as he hurried by and headed directly for the cardiac care unit. As he approached the nurse's station, there was only one person from the Department left, Detective Halifax. He was speaking with a nurse and looking pale.

Hal turned and looked at Charles with a combination of pain and dread. Charles hung back at first and didn't speak. He didn't want to hear what he feared Halifax was about to say. Reluctantly, he walked up to the desk, and Hal placed his hand on Charles' shoulder. "He's gone, Charlie." The younger man blinked away tears.

The color drained from the older man's face, and he felt momentarily unsteady. "Gone?" he repeated. "You mean he didn't make it?" Charles asked incredulously, feeling temporarily disoriented. The full impact of Hal's words finally sunk in, and Charles knew he had to pull himself together for Hal. Although Charles and Matt had been friends for three decades, young Halifax had looked to the man as a mentor, and possibly even as a father figure. The loss was great for him too.

Detective Halifax nodded, then closed his eyes and shook his head in disbelief. The two men stood silently together for a few moments until Charles finally spoke. "What about the arrangements?" he asked, looking first at Hal and then at the nurse.

"The Department is handling everything," Hal replied. "I just spoke with the Chief."

The two men left the hospital together without speaking. "Could you give me a ride back to the station?" Hal asked when they reached the parking lot. "I just remembered that I told Gallagher to take my car when I thought …" He didn't finish the sentence, but Charles knew the man had expected to be by Matt's side that day just as he had.

"You coming in?" Hal asked when they pulled up in front of the station.

"No, I don't think I can take it today."

Hal got out and thanked Charles, adding, "Sorry, sir."

"Me too."

As the detective walked away, Charles called to him. "Would you let the Chief know I'd like to be involved in the service in any way he thinks is appropriate—casket watch, pallbearer, whatever they need. There's no family, you know."

"There's you and me, Charlie. Matt's been like a father to me," he added, his voice catching as he looked away.

* * * * *

Sarah heard the car pull into the garage and was surprised that Charles was returning so soon. She had expected him to be at the hospital most of the day.

When she saw his face, she knew.

Chapter 17

"Hal, it's Charlie Parker. I'd like to see you."

It had been several weeks since the funeral and Charles was just getting to the point where he could begin to focus on other things. The loss had been profound and painful for him, but his friends and family had been a great comfort to him. Today he felt ready to revisit the Waterford girl's murder.

"Come on over, Charlie," the detective responded. "I'll be in the office for another hour or two."

When he arrived, Charles pulled a chair over near Hal and spoke in a confidential tone, saying, "Hal, I know the Department doesn't want me involved in active cases, but I want to help you solve the Waterford case. I owe it to Matt."

"Yeah, I feel that way too," the detective responded. "That case was the final nail in his coffin. Lieutenant Gibson's been transferred in from Deep Lake to take Matt's place, and that means he's got the case. They're keeping me on it and, as you can imagine, it's a political nightmare for him already. He said he's getting calls from the Chief, the Mayor, our congressmen, and the all the newspapers between here and Tennessee—and after every one of those calls, he calls me."

Charles shook his head, remembering the pressures that came with the political cases, and almost everything these days was turned into a political case. "I'd like your help, Charlie, but we'll have to keep it under wraps."

They discussed the logistics and agreed to get together that evening at the Parkers' house. It was Sarah's quilt club night, so they'd have the house to themselves.

As he was driving home, Charles thought about his friend's funeral and the impressive turnout of Matt's fellow officers. Many took the opportunity to speak, paying their respect to this esteemed officer whom they consistently described as competent and thorough in his work, fair and consistent with his officers, and admired by his friends. Charles started to stand, but felt that what he had to say was too personal. He wanted to thank Matt for his friendship, his mentoring in the early days, for sharing his pain when his first wife died, and for making it possible for him to continue to be involved in department cases from time to time after he retired.

Instead of driving directly home, Charles turned into Green Knolls Cemetery and knelt by his friend's grave. Tears ran down his cheeks as he poured out his heart and requested his friend's forgiveness for never having said these things to him while he was alive.

"He knew," Sarah said to him later that day. "Just like you know he cared about you."

* * * * *

Sarah had prepared a tray of cheese and crackers before she left and Charles had just handed Hal a beer. "Why don't you start," Charlie said. "Where is the Department on this case?"

"Okay, well first I'd like to catch you up on a few things that the Department has been working on—things I don't think Matt shared with you." He went on to explain that they had projected the most likely route Darius had driven in order to reach the location where the body was found near Nashville. "We've faxed pictures and requested that local departments take a look at diners and truck stops along the way to see if anyone remembers anything."

"Any luck?"

"Not yet, but we're hopeful. There's no way we can force the local jurisdictions to investigate on our behalf, and Headquarters hasn't released funds for our own men to go down."

"At least, not yet," Charles interjected, knowing that funds became available in direct correlation to the degree of political pressure.

"True, but for now, we're at the mercy of these local jurisdictions."

"Okay," Charles responded. "I have some information to share with you as well, and Matt wasn't aware of any of this. A small group of friends here in the village have gotten together to do some local legwork. They've interviewed friends of the girl and have been able to track her to the moment she left town with Darius."

Charles had borrowed Sophie's card file for the meeting, and he went on to give the detective all the names of the people they had spoken with and the information they had been able to compile as a result.

"Impressive," the detective commented, making a few notes of his own. "There may be some useful leads in here. We'll get right on it. I want our boys to talk to every one of these kids."

They spent another hour going over the various theories the group had come up with as well as a few ideas the Department had developed. The detective assured Charles that the investigators would take a serious look at everything but went on to admit that the Department felt that Darius Mitchell was the most likely perpetrator. "Most of the Department's efforts are concentrated on finding him."

The detective went on to say, "There's the fingerprints, Charlie, and he had opportunity—the body was found in his car—at least the car he stole. The guy's a loser with a record, he's already wanted for a felony, and there's that bench warrant hanging out there. All we really have to his credit is the blind faith of his ex-foster mother."

"I know, Hal, and I appreciate that you're willing to listen to other points of view. We may all be misguided by this woman's perception, but my gut tells me it wasn't him. Over the years, I've learned to trust that feeling. It's been right far more often than it's been wrong."

After an evening of serious brainstorming about the case intermixed with getting to know one another on a more personal level, the two men were relaxing with a beer when Sarah returned.

"So, what have you detectives been up to tonight?" Sarah asked as she hung her jacket in the hall closet. The men were still sitting in the living room with an empty platter between them and several beer bottles on their side tables. "You couldn't give your guest a glass?" she needled her husband.

"Real men don't drink beer from glasses," Charles joshed in return.

"Well, there's a lady present now, so I'm getting you both glasses."

"Not for me," Hal said standing up and reaching for his coat, which he had tossed on the couch. Sarah gave Charles another disapproving look when she realized he hadn't offered to take his guest's coat. "I've got an early day tomorrow," Hal continued. Turning to Charles, he said, "Thanks for sharing all this information with me, Charlie, and tell that friend of yours that her 3″ by 5″ card file was extremely helpful."

"She'll love hearing that," Sarah responded."

"So how was your quilt club meeting?" Charles asked as he closed the front door.

"We always have a great time, but I'd rather hear about your meeting with the detective. Did you learn anything?"

"I think he learned more than I did, actually," Charles confessed. "The police have honed in on Darius as the killer, and most of their efforts seem to be directed toward finding him."

"But the paper said he's only a person of interest."

"Same thing, essentially. They can't accuse him at this point."

"So," Sarah concluded, "this only means we have to work faster and smarter. If we don't find out who killed the girl, then no one will, and Darius will be convicted."

"Sarah, have you considered that he just might have killed the girl?"

"Charles, I've told you before that I trust Bernice's judgment. She has known him most of his life, and she knows he couldn't have done this heinous crime."

"Sarah, your friend who, by the way, you've only known for a couple of months, only recently became somewhat realistic about her foster son's past criminal behavior. How can we really trust her judgment about him now?"

"I thought you told me that your instincts tell you he didn't do it."

"Well," he responded tentatively, "I guess I'm just beginning to question my instincts."

"Aren't they usually right?"

"They were," he responded.

But can I still trust them? he asked himself, but not aloud. *I'm getting old, I've had strokes with neurological damage, it's been more than ten years since I was actively in the field. What if I'm wrong?*

"You can't fool me, Charles," Sarah responded to his silence. "I can always tell when you're having a serious discussion with yourself and those one-sided talks of yours are never productive. You need to be communicating your thoughts to another person. Tell me what's going on."

"Okay. I was thinking that perhaps my age and health have affected my investigative instincts."

"Nonsense," she responded, brushing him aside with a dismissive hand gesture and walking out of the room.

"Well," he muttered to himself sarcastically, "So much for the benefits of communicating my thoughts." He shook his head with a chuckle, turned off the light, and followed his wife out of the room.

* * * * *

There was a tapping at Sarah's kitchen door while she was making coffee the next morning. "Who's there?" she called out, and Barney immediately ran into the kitchen barking.

"It's just me," Sophie called out. "Tell that dog it's a friend."

"It's okay, Barney," Sarah said, holding his collar as she unlocked the door. They weren't accustomed to people knocking at the kitchen door since it only opened into the garage. "How did you get into the garage?" she asked, looking out and seeing that the garage door was raised. "Oh, I guess Charles forgot to close it," she said as she pushed the control button and it automatically lowered.

"This is a surprise," she said. Her friend had obviously walked from her house and was carrying a small tote bag. "Come on in. Coffee's on."

"I'm trying to get more exercise. Norman wants to drive back down to the cabin this weekend and check out some of the nature sites in the park."

"The park?"

"Well, I haven't learned just what to call it, but it's all those recreational and nature areas between the lakes."

"Ah, the Land Between the Lakes. And you're going, I assume."

"Would I miss it?"

"He wants to go to the planetarium for sure, and he's talking about this working farm where everyone is in original nineteenth-century clothing, and they've kept everything authentic. I figure I'll see some vintage quilts while I'm there."

"I didn't realize they have a planetarium. I always loved to visit the one in Chicago with my parents," Sarah reminisced.

"I don't think it'll be as fancy as the Adler, but they have shows on the constellations and black holes, stuff like that. He wants to go over to their observatory where you can look through these strong telescopes. He's excited about it, and I'll enjoy being with him. I'm looking forward to the nineteenth-century farm myself."

"And being with Norman?"

Sophie giggled. "And being with Norman."

"Will his family be there?"

"Not this time," Sophie said coyly.

"I see," Sarah teased, and Sophie blushed.

Sarah poured their coffee and set the cookie jar on the table. "These are the real ones," she assured Sophie who was always afraid she'd accidentally get one of Charles' nonfat, sugar-free cookies. "So what do you have in your tote bag?" Sarah asked, hoping to see one of Sophie's latest quilting projects.

"These are the 3″ by 5″ cards. I was afraid something might happen while I'm away and you wouldn't have access to our records."

Sarah smiled. Her friend took her documentation responsibility very seriously.

"I'm glad you brought them, but we probably won't be needing them this weekend."

"Weekend? Didn't I tell you? We're going to be gone for a week, maybe longer!"

"Really? That's a surprise. What about Emma?"

"Oh, she's going too. It's a little family vacation, but I think the main reason Norman wants to go right now is that this is the best time to see the bald eagles. He has a thing about eagles. In fact, he's got me watching the eagle cam."

"What's an eagle cam?" Sarah asked.

"It's a camera set to observe an eagle's nest twenty-four hours a day. You watch on the computer. I've seen the mother and father taking turns sitting on the eggs and once I saw babies breaking out of their shells. Once the nest was full of fish. Then one day when I went online to see how they were doing, everyone was gone. I was actually sad, and I find myself wondering if the babies made it okay. Anyway," she added looking embarrassed about revealing her soft side, "I can see how he got hooked."

Changing the subject, Sophie asked, "Where's Charles today?"

"He was on his computer all morning, when he suddenly hurried through the house, gave me a quick peck on the cheek, and said he needed to see Detective Halifax."

"Have you met this fellow?"

"Yes, he came here to talk to Charles a week or so ago while you and I were at the quilt club. He seems to be open to the idea that Darius might be innocent, at least of the murder."

"But he's with the police department. Why would he be working with Charles to prove it's someone else?"

"Charles told me that the detective was raised by his mother. His father was with the department and was killed in the line of duty when Hal was only eight. Lieutenant Stokely, Charles' previous supervisor …"

"The man that just died?"

"Yes," Sarah responded, looking distressed. "It's been hard on Charles. Anyway, Matt brought Detective Halifax into the department a few years ago and mentored him. Charles thinks the young man might have seen Matt as a father figure. …"

"Do you think he might be transferring some of that on to Charles?"

"Interesting thought. I think it's possible."

"Well, he couldn't pick a better role model."

Sarah smiled. "I agree."

* * * * *

"Come on in, Charlie, but close the door," Detective Halifax said rather formally when Charles arrived. Charles could see his desk was covered with file folders and he was frantically making notes. He finally pushed the yellow pad aside, sighed, and looked at Charles.

"What's up?" he asked.

It took a moment for Charles to respond as his thoughts went back to the many times he stood before Matt, seeing his friend lost in his work and reluctant to break his stride just as Hal was doing. He had to shake the memory out of his head before he could speak.

"I know you're busy, Hal, and I'm sorry to barge in, but I've been looking into the girl's father's background. Did you know that Waterford was a prosecuting attorney before he got into politics?"

"I heard something about that. What are you thinking?"

"Do you suppose one of the dirt bags he prosecuted might have …"

"A revenge killing?" Hal responded, jumping way ahead. "You think some guy he prosecuted came after him?" the detective asked doubtfully.

"I think it's possible...." Charles responded defensively.

"But his daughter, Charlie? Why his daughter? Why not Waterford himself?"

"I suppose the guy could have figured losing his daughter would cause Waterford the most pain?" Charles replied, beginning to doubt the theory himself.

"I don't know, Charlie," Hal added shaking his head. "This sounds pretty farfetched. I need to munch on it for a while. I'll give you a call."

As he was returning home, Charles saw Sophie slowly walking away from his house. He pulled over and called to her, "Hey, cutie, want a ride?"

"Do I ever!" she responded, walking much faster once she was heading for his car.

"What are you doing on foot today anyway?" he asked as he circled past his own house which sat on the cul-de-sac and drove the few blocks to Sophie's house.

She told him about the trip and her crash plan to get in shape before they left.

"Not the way it works, my dear," Charles responded. "You could end up too sore to enjoy the trip if you overdo it."

"Thanks, Charles. I needed an excuse to stop this craziness. Will you come in for pie? It's real," she added as an enticement.

"Can't do it, Sophie. Those tests the doc ran last week showed lots of plaque building up. I may need surgery, but we're going to try changing my meds first. In the meantime, I've got to be on a rigid diet and increase my workouts."

"Sorry Charles, and I won't try to tempt you. We need you to stay with us. You probably heard the ambulance the other night? Sam Blackstone is gone, just like that. I don't know what'll become of his wife. He was her caregiver, and there's no other family. She'll probably end up over at the nursing home."

Charles sat with the car running, thinking about the Blackstones. It was suddenly very easy to turn down Sophie's pie.

"Have a great trip, Sophie," he said as she was getting out of the car.

"Oh," she turned and added, "Sarah has all the 3″ by 5″ cards in case you folks need them."

"Thanks, Sophie," he responded, smiling inside. *Such a special lady.*

As he walked into his own house, Sarah said, "Did I just see you picking up a woman off the street?"

"You did at that," he responded giving her a gentle pat. "Thank you for taking such good care of my diet," he added more seriously.

"I plan to keep you around," she responding, realizing that Sophie must have told him about the Blackstones.

Chapter 18

"Come on, Charles. We need to leave, or we'll be late."

"Late?" he responded, temporarily forgetting their commitment.

"Late for serving dinner," she replied in a slightly impatient tone. Sarah had assured Sophie that she and Charles would cover for her and Norman at her church's dinner for the homeless.

"I don't know how to do this," Charles complained as he drove into town.

"It's easy. You just scoop up food, plop it on a plate, and pass it to the next person in line. I'll make sure you get mashed potato duty, okay? You know how to serve mashed potatoes, don't you?"

"I suppose. Do I get to eat?"

"You certainly may if you want, or we can stop off at La Bonita's afterward. Bernice and Andy love it there. It's romantic. ..." she added flirtatiously.

"Well, how can I resist. Okay, I'll scoop mashed potatoes if it will earn me a Tex-Mex meal with enchiladas and ..."

"Hold it," Sarah interrupted. "I don't think they'll have anything you can eat right now. The doctor said you can have those things once in a while after they get your numbers down, but you've only been on the new medication for a couple of weeks."

"How about chili? That can't be too bad, can it?"

"Hmm," she responded thoughtfully. "Beans are good, and the sauce would be okay. I wonder if they offer it with chicken instead of beef."

"This is discouraging," Charles responded. "Those mashed potatoes are starting to sound just fine."

"How about this. If they don't offer any chicken dishes, we'll ask them to make you a taco salad with lots of extra lettuce and tomatoes, less chili, and no cheese."

"And I still get the romantic atmosphere?"

"Absolutely," she responded, "and a glass of red wine."

"I'm game," he agreed.

When they arrived at the church, there was already a line waiting for the doors to open. Charles drove around to the back and unloaded two Crock-Pots filled with green beans that had simmered all day with onions and ham. "Where do I put these?"

"I'll show you. Sophie brought me over before she left and taught me the ropes. It will be easy. There are people in charge. We're just here to serve."

"Scoop potatoes, right?"

"Right."

"Hi, I'm Reverend George," the young preacher said. "You must be the Parkers." Sarah wondered how he knew but soon realized that everyone else was there and at their stations. Reverend George led them to their spots, Charles in front of a tray of yellow squash and Sarah next to him serving meat loaf.

"These aren't potatoes. How do I do it?" Charles said, feigning incompetence.

"Just like potatoes," Sarah assured him. "One heaping scoop on each plate and some people might say they don't want any, and others might ask what it is."

"And it is …?"

"Squash, Charles. Squash," she responded impatiently. "Have you ever been in a kitchen?"

"I have a wife for things like that," he responded, and she shot him a look that could kill until she noticed the sly grin on his face and realized he was teasing her.

"You've served at these dinners before, I assume?" he asked in a more serious tone.

"Not here, but yes. It's been years. The church we went to back home offered dinners too." She realized she was still thinking of the place she raised her children as home. She glanced at Charles, hoping she hadn't hurt his feelings, but he was happily talking with the man coming through the line.

"You're sure you don't want any? It's squash, you know," he was saying with authority, "and delicious." He winked at his wife and went on to the next person in line.

* * * * *

"Sophie," Sarah exclaimed. "I was wondering if we'd hear from you today."

"I just wanted to make sure everything worked out at the church dinner last night. How was Charles with it?"

"He was reluctant at first, but he had a great time in the end. He even recognized a couple of the older guys and stayed late to talk with them. Are you having a good time?"

"A fantastic time," Sophie responded. "We've been at the cabin for the last couple of days just relaxing, but today we went out for a ride through some of the surrounding small towns and here's the exciting part. We stopped for lunch, and there was a consignment shop across the street with the cutest little sewing machine you ever saw in the window."

"A little machine?" Sarah questioned. "Do you know what kind?"

"It's a Singer and comes with a case and everything. It only weighs eleven pounds and would be perfect for taking to the meetings, but I don't know if they're asking too much. Is Charles home? Maybe he could check on his computer."

"He's right here. Charles," Sarah called to him. "Sophie wants to speak to you."

Sophie told him about the machine as he headed for his computer. "Okay, you say it's called a Featherweight?" Charles responded.

"Yes, a Singer Featherweight. It's just a little machine and would be perfect for carrying around, and it looks easy enough to use. It doesn't have all those scary buttons and switches and blinking lights that Sarah's has." As she was talking, she could hear the tapping of his fingers on the keyboard.

"Okay, here are a bunch of them for sale. Do you know what year it was made?"

"The man is checking now. Do you see the prices?"

"Yes, here's one for $52 that looks like it was run over by a semi," he responded with a chuckle. "And here's one for $279 that is dated 1957, but it doesn't look too good either. What are they asking?"

"$399," she responded. "Does that seem high?"

"The $279 one doesn't have a case or accessories," Charles added.

"This one has both. Keep looking at prices."

"Okay, here's one but it's sold. Too bad you missed it. It was in mint condition and had the emblem for the 1933 Chicago World Fair, and it sold for just $3,200," he teased.

"Charles, be serious. Should I pay $399 for this one? The man just told me that its birthdate is 1948."

"Birthdate?" Charles questioned. "Are we still talking about a sewing machine?"

"Yes," Sophie chuckled. "The proprietor said it's tradition to refer to the year a Featherweight was built as its birthdate."

"Okay, let me reword my search for ones with a 1948 birthday."

Sophie waited eagerly while Charles checked out several sources.

"Okay, I can find them from $250 to $550, depending on the condition and what comes with them. How does this one look?"

"It looks excellent, Charles. I don't see a scratch on it, and even the case is in good condition."

"And does it have attachments?"

"Yes, the case has lots of doodads inside. Sarah will know what they are," Sophie added confidently.

"Well, looking at the ones for sale online, I see a really nice one here for $499 and another for $425. And there's the one for $550 I mentioned earlier, but I think it's probably overpriced. There are several others in the $200 to low

$300 range, but they have scratches, and the cases are pretty worn looking. One doesn't have any attachments. What did you say he's asking?"

"$399," Sophie replied.

"Are you on speaker?" Charles asked.

"No, I'm outside. Why?"

"Well, the machine that you're describing is on these websites at the higher end of the range. I'd say it's a great deal at $399, but why don't you try to get him to come down. Did you make sure it operates?"

"I don't know how to use it, but Sarah will teach me. The salesman sewed a few stitches and showed them to me. I looked at both sides just like Sarah does and the stitches looked fine to me."

"Is Norman with you?"

"No, he walked up the street to the hardware store. I was just waiting here when I spotted this machine in the window. Should I wait for him?"

"No, why don't you see what kind of deal you can make with this guy. You probably stand a better chance on your own, especially if he doesn't spot Norman's Mercedes."

"Thanks, Charles. Tell Sarah I'll let her know how it works out."

Several hours later, the phone rang again, and Charles could see it was Sophie, so he handed it to Sarah without answering.

"Sophie, did you get it?"

"I sure did. Tell Charles we compromised at $375, and it's in the car. I can hardly wait to show it to you."

"Charles wanted me to ask you if your new Featherweight came with an instruction manual."

"Oh my," Sophie responded sounding worried. "I didn't see anything like that, and I didn't think to ask. I just figured you'd know how to use it. Don't you?"

"I've never used one, but the reason Charles wanted me to ask you is that he found a 1948 Featherweight manual online. He'll order it for you."

"Thank you, Sarah. How much was it?"

"It's our gift in exchange for you letting me play with your new toy."

They were both excited as Sarah told her friend some of the things Charles had learned during his computer searches. "After he talked to you, he learned that the Singer Featherweight was introduced at the Chicago World's Fair in 1933."

"Ah, that explains the three thousand dollar one," Sophie responded. "A real collector's item."

"He said that some quilters collect Featherweights just about as compulsively as they collect fabric."

"You mean this might just be the beginning?" Sophie responded with an excited chuckle.

"He said this will be a good investment, too. They are highly valued by collectors, especially in good working condition."

"Well, I just wanted something light enough to take to the meetings. I didn't realize I was joining a cult. Besides, I bought it mostly because it was so cute!"

Sarah laughed. Her friend had a history of being attracted to things that were miniaturized. She had an antique wooden printer's tray hanging on her wall filled with an assortment of tiny china collectibles.

"When are you coming home?" Sarah asked.

"We'll be back early next week. Have the Sleuths had a meeting?"

"No, we're waiting for you."

"Okay, go ahead and plan it for Wednesday night at my house," Sophie responded. "I found a bakery down here that sells … well, just wait and see," she teased.

"It sounds like you're having a good time," Sarah chuckled, and her friend was quiet for a moment.

When Sophie finally responded, she spoke in a softened tone. "Sarah, I had no idea that I could ever be this happy again."

"What's going on?" Charles asked when he noticed his wife's satisfied smile.

"My friend is in love. …"

Chapter 19

"We haven't accomplished anything," Sophie was complaining. The group was meeting at her house and were crowded around the kitchen table. Emma, Sophie's white mixed-breed rescue, had checked out each guest individually, and apparently they had all passed her test. She was now curled up in the corner of the kitchen on the old blanket Sarah had brought her. Emma loved it because it smelled like Sarah's Barney.

"What do you mean, Sophie?" Andy responded. "We've talked to Courtney's friends, and we've tracked her movements up to the moment she left town, and we confirmed she left with Darius."

"We even know why she left with him," Norman added. "She wanted him to take her to Tennessee to see a guy she met on the internet."

"But we don't know what happened to her or why," Sophie continued, "and we haven't cleared Darius."

Sarah could tell that Charles wanted to say something, but was holding back. "Go ahead," she whispered. "Put it out there if it's the way you feel."

Charles sighed as the group turned to look at him. "Okay, first of all, I wanted to let everyone know that I've been talking with Detective Halifax and offered our help with the case. I told him about what we've done here, and he said he'd follow up on our leads, but he also said that the Department is convinced Darius is their man."

Glancing at Bernice to gauge her reaction, he continued. "They've got his fingerprints on the car and on the girl. He had opportunity, and he's gone into hiding. In addition to that, they're looking at his history and past behavior, his juvie record, his felony arrest, possible credit card fraud, and the Failure to Appear charge."

Charles turned and looked at Bernice saying, "Bernice, forgive me for what I'm going to say now, but it needs to be said."

Bernice, her back rigid and her jaw clenched in preparation for bad news, nodded for him to continue.

"I have to ask the question. Do we know for sure that this young man *didn't* kill the girl?"

"No, we don't know that," Andy responded immediately. "What we do know is that no one is making any effort other than this group to look at alternative theories. We live in a country where a man is innocent until proven guilty, at least that's what we profess. When they find Darius, and they will, he will be tried, and there will be no one to offer an alternative theory. Darius will be prosecuted, and maybe he did do it, but maybe he didn't, and who is looking at that possibility? No one but us as far as I can see."

"Won't his lawyer do that?" Sophie asked.

"Do you think a court-appointed lawyer will spend the time to track down all these alternative theories?"

"The reality is that we probably won't solve the girl's murder, but," Norman added, "we can provide the lawyer with enough theories to create doubt in the minds of the jurors."

"Okay, is this what we're saying then?" Charles clarified. "We don't need to know whether or not he's innocent. We want to ensure that he can have a fair trial."

"Yes," Norman said. "I think we should stop thinking about whether the police are right or wrong. We need to develop alternative suspects for the murder or Darius will be left holding the bag, even if he's innocent."

"I don't know how to get all this on a 3″ by 5″ card," Sophie announced and everyone laughed. As usual, Sophie broke the tension in the room.

"Just write down on one card that the Undercover Sleuths assume Darius to be innocent because it's the American way," Andy said.

Sophie brought the second pot of coffee to the table and asked with a twinkle in her eye if anyone would like a treat with their coffee.

"Stop teasing, Sophie," Sarah announced. "You told me you were bringing us something special from Kentucky."

Sophie returned to the counter and uncovered a platter of cream-colored confections, which caused exclamations of joy from her guests.

"What is it, Sophie?" Andy asked. "It looks decadent."

"These are coconut pecan pralines," Sophie replied proudly, still holding the platter just out of her guest's reach. "The baker told me it's a traditional handmade southern candy made with sugar, nuts, and cream. These, of course, have coconut as well, and I can tell you that they are to die for!"

"And she knows what she's talking about," Norman teased. "She sampled them several times a day while we were in Kentucky. We had to go back to the bakery to replenish our supply in order to bring some home."

"You didn't do so bad yourself," Sophie replied, tapping the little bulge just above his belt. Setting the platter down in the middle of the table, she said, "Go at it, folks, and let me know how you like them."

Bernice made a swooning sound with her first bite, the men all reached for seconds within moments of eating their first one, and Sophie sat back and grinned with satisfaction. "I knew you'd like these," she chuckled.

Sarah gave Charles a look of concern when he started to reach for this third, and he pulled his hand back reluctantly. She smiled her appreciation, and he gave her an understanding wink as he reached for his coffee instead.

Once they were satiated, Sophie asked, "So what do we need to do tonight?"

"We've already done one thing," Norman said, assuming his role as leader of the group. "We've clearly defined our role. Has anyone had other thoughts over the past week?"

Charles waited to see if anyone else had anything before he spoke again. He didn't want to monopolize the meeting, but he wanted to share what he'd learned about Waterford's background as a prosecutor and the possible implications.

"This is an interesting idea, Charles," Andy responded. "How could we check this out?"

"I passed this information on to Detective Halifax and I hope he'll investigate it. He was reluctant at first, but he called a few days ago and said he'd look into it. He's in a much better position than we are to get that kind of information."

"Do you think he really will?" Bernice asked.

"I think he wants to get to the truth. He feels a responsibility to clear this case for Matt. He was very close to Lieutenant Stokely."

"We're so sorry about that, Charles. How are you doing?" Norman asked.

"It's been rough, but I'm okay. I'm just sorry I didn't go fishing with Matt when he asked me."

"When was that?" Sarah asked with surprise. She hadn't heard about the invitation.

"Every spring and summer for the last fifteen or twenty years," Charles responded regretfully. "And I was always too busy."

"Let that be a lesson to us all," Andy responded.

* * * * *

Everyone had left except Sarah and Charles. The three friends sat around the table looking discouraged. "Sophie's right you know, Charles. We really haven't done anything that will help Darius' case. I feel like we're letting Bernice down."

"I guess you're right," Charles responded. "It seems like we've identified lots of alternative theories about how this girl might have been killed, but we haven't been able to prove any of them. Of course, we shouldn't have to if the police would just follow up on our leads. I took our ideas to Matt in the past and now to Halifax, but I don't have much faith that they've look into any of them very seriously."

"Before you leave," Sophie added, standing up and bringing her card file back to the table, "do you think we could take a quick look at my cards and clarify who we think might have been involved? With that little mini-vacation of ours, I've lost track of just where we are."

"Sure," Charles said, but his voice seemed flat and discouraged. "Actually, I need a refresher myself, and I didn't even have a vacation."

"Okay, so here are the theories we've considered." Sophie began jotting down notes on a sheet of paper as she thumbed through her cards and talked. "One, someone on Capello's campaign, maybe even Capello himself, kidnapped the girl or had her kidnapped, in hopes of distracting her father who is running against him. Maybe it was just meant to be a kidnapping and something went wrong," she added. "Then two, and I'm not sure we talked much about this one, but maybe they picked up a crazy hitchhiker."

Sarah sighed, and Sophie continued. "A third theory is that the jealous boyfriend caught up with them, and four, those two escaped convicts got to them." She stopped reading and looked up. "Do I need to say more about the escaped convict theory?"

"No," Charles responded. "Go on."

I only have two more cards. Our fifth idea was that it could have been a revenge killing by someone Waterford convicted back when he was a prosecutor, and our sixth idea was that it could have simply been a random killing, and we'll never know who did it."

"When you lay it out like this, Sophie, there seem to be lots of possibilities but not much we can do to prove any of them," Sarah responded, sounding discouraged.

"When I hear them listed out like this," Charles said, suddenly smiling, "I'm encouraged because I realize that there are already things being done. We've identified her friends, including the boyfriend, and the police have all the information we collected, and they said they would follow up. The Department has requested that local jurisdictions all the way from here to Tennessee check out places they may have stopped and get whatever information they can. There's a manhunt going on for the escaped convicts, and they're sure to catch them and perhaps learn something from them if they were involved. As for Capello …"

"Yes?" Sarah spoke up raising an eyebrow. "Are you reconsidering about Sophie and me joining the campaign and nosing around?"

"We'll talk about it," he responded unenthusiastically.

"What about the revenge killing idea?" Sophie asked.

"Halifax is looking into some of the most controversial cases Waterford prosecuted. He's looking for any threats that were made and any convicts recently released. He wasn't impressed with the idea at first, but he's beginning to sound more interested in that route. He told me yesterday that his new boss is listening to this one as well."

"Okay, I'm feeling a little better," Sophie was saying when the phone rang.

"Norman, it's past midnight. What are you doing up?" She knew he was an early riser, but was usually in bed by 10:00. She listened for a moment as he apparently told her the reason for his late-night call.

"Sure I have his number, but he and Sarah are right here. Do you want to talk to him?"

Sophie handed the phone to Charles who listened for a moment and then said, "Hold on, Norman. Do you mind if I put you on speaker?"

Charles pushed the speaker button and said, "Okay, go ahead."

"Well, what I was saying was that I had a thought on the way home—something we haven't looked at."

"What's that?" Sophie called from across the kitchen.

"We haven't talked about this person the Waterford girl was going down to Tennessee to meet. We only have her friends' word that he wanted her to come. Maybe they got there and maybe the guy is crazy, or married, or heck, any number of things. She'd never met the man, and we don't know anything about him. She may have walked into a very bad situation."

"Norman," Charles responded enthusiastically. "You may be on to something. I'll call Hal first thing in the morning and run this past him. And I think they need to see if any of her friends have the guy's name. In fact, I'll ask Hal if he wants us to make another visit to the café and ask more questions."

"Good idea. The kids opened up to Andy and Sarah before. Let's send them again."

"Yes," Charles responded thoughtfully, "and I think I'll go too, but I won't let on I'm with them. I might pick up some body language if I can just watch from across the room. Say, while I've got you on the phone, Sarah and Sophie are asking again about volunteering for Capello's campaign. Any new thoughts on that one?"

"I don't think we can stop them, Charles, but I hope they don't do it. Tell them I believe that it's much too dangerous."

"We can hear you," Sophie announced. "We're just thinking about it. Nothing's decided."

"Charles, maybe you and I should do it," Norman suggested.

"Not me, Norman. Even retired, I can't seem to hide the fact that I'm a cop. I was never able to go undercover when I was on the force—I was always spotted right away. If Capello is actually mob-connected, they'll pick me out in a minute. Matt was going to put someone in there undercover, but I don't know if he ever did. I'll ask Halifax tomorrow."

"So why are you folks there so late?" Norman asked. Charles told him what they'd been doing.

"We should have done that during our meeting," Norman responded. "It would help all of us to review where we stand."

"Sophie's written it all down. I'll take it home and make copies for our next get-together," Charles responded. "We're heading home now. Here's your girl," he added as he handed the phone back to Sophie. She disappeared around the corner to say good night privately, and Sarah and Charles began clearing the table and stacking the plates and mugs on the sink.

"Good night, Sophie," they called to their friend as they were leaving.

Chapter 20

"Do I ever have something to show you folks," Sophie announced as she breezed into the quilt club meeting just late enough to make a dramatic entrance. She was carrying a black box, which she placed on the table. "You'll never guess what I have!"

"A Featherweight?" Kimberly asked, and Sophie's face fell. "How did you know?" she asked.

"I'd know that black case anywhere," Kimberly chuckled. "Now show us what you have."

Sophie pulled the Featherweight out of the case and set it down on the table proudly. "My first sewing machine," she announced.

"Where did you get it?" several members of the club asked almost in unison.

Sophie told the story of how she discovered the little machine while everyone in the group crowded around her. "Such excitement," Sophie commented. "It's just a little sewing machine."

"It's more than that," Ruth commented. "Quilters love Featherweights, and this is a particularly nice one, Sophie," she added as she examined the machine. She tilted it over and looked at the serial number. "This was made around 1948?" she asked, but seemed to already know the answer.

"How could you tell?" Sophie asked. "The man at the store told me that, but I couldn't find the date on the machine anywhere."

"I could tell by the serial number. Yours begins with AH and those were made in 1947 and 1948."

"I'm going home to look at my serial numbers," Kimberly responded.

"'Numbers' plural?" Sophie asked. "You have more than one?"

"Sure. We've been collecting them for years," Kimberly responded, looking toward her sister, Christina, for confirmation.

"Our mother left us one of the very first ones that Singer produced," Christina replied. "They came out in 1933 and Mom bought hers the next year. Then she got another one a few years later for us girls to share, but we kept fighting over it, so she got the third one. I guess that started our collection," she added, looking at her sister. "We still have those three."

"That got us started, but we continued on our own," Kimberly admitted. "I recently found a white one that we both love using."

"I thought they were only black," Sarah responded, having looked at some of the ones Charles had found online.

Delores spoke up, "The most common color is shiny black like you have, Sophie, but they made them in a black crinkle during the war which is sometimes called *matte*. I think they were made for the military, in fact."

"And they also came in tan and white, but those came along later."

"When did the white ones come out?" someone asked.

"Around 1964, and the white ones were all made in Scotland. I have one I can bring in next time if you'd like to see it," Delores offered.

"Why don't we all bring in our Featherweights next time," Ruth suggested. "How many of you have them?" Five of the members raised their hands, and Sophie suddenly shot her arm into the air, realizing she was now a Featherweight owner as well.

"Can I ask a question?" Caitlyn asked timidly.

"Sure, Caitlyn," Ruth responded gently, knowing that the young girl often felt shy in the group.

"Why would anyone want one of these when you already have those fancy machines with all the special stitches?"

Ruth laughed and nodded her understanding of the question. "I know, it's strange, isn't it? I guess it's just a quilter's desire to be part of the whole history of quilting. When this machine came out in 1933, it was a real break-through. Singer had introduced machines made of aluminum instead of cast iron. They only weighed eleven pounds, and suddenly women could take their sewing machines to class or to their friend's houses."

"I saw an ad in a vintage sewing book," Delores added, "that referred to the Featherweight as 'the Perfect Portable.'"

"Do they still make them?" Caitlyn asked, beginning to show interest in the little machine.

"No, they stopped production in 1968 or '69, I believe," Ruth responded. "It was about that time that women began to want a zigzag stitch and some of the other features they were coming out with."

"And people still use them?" Caitlyn asked curiously. She had moved up by Sophie's machine, gently touching the handwheel.

"We use ours," Christina responded.

"Me too," Delores added. "I love using it. I'm usually making a quilt, and the straight stitch is exactly what I need and that little machine of mine just purrs along."

"They're easy to service," Ruth added. "I can't do any service on my fancy machine, but it's simple to keep the Featherweight going. I do it all myself with an oil can and my worn-out manual."

"And they are extremely reliable," Delores added. "I think it's because they were made back in the day when things were made to last."

Ruth laughed. "They hadn't invented the concept of 'planned obsolescence' yet. These machines were made to be passed down from one generation to the next."

While everyone talked, Sophie sat with her arms cradling her new Featherweight as it sat on the table in front of her. She smiled with pride and excitement.

"There's another reason I use mine," Kimberly spoke up with a melancholy look. "It makes me feel a part of a very special tradition. It's hard to explain, but it gives me a feeling of connection to all the women that came before me, especially the ones that owned my little Featherweight."

As Sarah listened, she began to imagine having one herself. She had purchased her machine with all the bells and whistles and certainly loved it, but it was too heavy to bring to class, so she usually just used one of Ruth's machines for club projects or did her sewing at home between meetings. *I wonder …*

The group continued to chat about their machines until Ruth suggested they get started on their project. The members had been making baby quilts for a local church that provided supplies to young mothers in need. Allison pulled two completed crib quilts out of her tote bag, and everyone complimented her on her work. She had used shades of green and yellow to make pinwheels on a white background. "I made them for a boy or a girl," she commented.

"I didn't get mine finished," Caitlyn explained as she held up half of a finished quilt top. She had chosen a fabric featuring kittens, and everyone loved the pattern she had chosen which involved fussy cutting the animals and placing them in the center of large Churn Dash blocks. "Do you think I could put flannel on the back, so it will be nice and soft for the baby?"

"You sure can," Ruth responded. "Just wash it like you did your other fabric, so you don't have to worry about it shrinking once it's on the quilt."

Most of the group spent the rest of the meeting cutting, sewing, and pressing, but Sophie and Delores moved to a side table where Delores taught her the basics of her new machine.

On their way home, Sarah asked how she was feeling about her new sewing machine, and Sophie responded, "I feel fantastic about it, and I'm ready to start planning a quilt for Norman. Will you help me?" she added almost shyly.

"You bet I will," Sarah responded with a wide grin. *My friend is officially a quilter—a quilter in love.*

* * * * *

"Charles, I've been thinking about my birthday …" Sarah had decided to ask him to find her a Featherweight.

"Me too," he responded.

Oh my, she thought. *He's already made his own plans for my birthday. I guess it's too late.*

"And I know what I'm getting for you."

"Oh?" she responded, trying to keep the disappointment out of her voice.

"In fact, I was hoping you'd help me find it since you know more about this sort of thing."

"Oh?" *Help him find it? Is it possible?* She could feel a mounting excitement.

"I got the idea from Norman," he added.

"Oh," she responded as her tone plummeted with disappointment. *Norman would probably suggest a party. …*

"Or would you rather I do it alone, so it'll be a surprise?"

"I feel like I'm on a roller coaster, Charles."

"That's exactly how you sound," he responded, looking confused. "Your voice goes up and then it goes down. What's going on?"

"Well, I was sort of hoping we could talk about looking for a Featherweight like Sophie has, but when you said …"

"I said Norman had an idea, and that is exactly what Norman suggested."

"No kidding?" she responded excitedly.

"He could see how excited Sophie was with it, and he thought you just might like to have one too."

"He came up with that? I'm amazed."

"Well," Charles added hesitantly, "I think Sophie may have had something to do with it as well."

"That makes more sense," Sarah responded laughing.

"So let's talk about it. I found several on the computer being sold on eBay, but that makes me a little nervous. I think you need to be able to try it out."

"I agree."

"So I was wondering about one of those local online classified advertisement websites. Individuals can advertise to sell things, buy things, provide services, find services, stuff like that. I was wondering if we should start there and restrict the responses to nearby locations so we can go see it."

"Not a bad idea," Sarah responded, "but I think we should talk to Ruth first. I know that some quilt shops sell them. She doesn't, but she might have an idea for us. I'm worried that we don't know enough about these machines, and we might end up buying the wrong one."

"Okay, but since this is going to be your birthday gift, let me do the legwork. I'll talk to her and see what I can track down, then the two of us will go look at them. Okay?"

"Okay. Now, I have a question for you. Have you spoken with Detective Halifax lately? I've been wondering if he's made any progress on any of the ideas you've taken to him."

"He has, as a matter of fact. I was just waiting for our next meeting to talk about it, but let me fill you in." As he was talking, he reached into the refrigerator for a bottle of Chardonnay and poured them each a glass. "Let's move into the living room."

Once they were settled, Charles told her about his meeting with the detective. "I was pleased to see that he was moving on some of our ideas. For one thing, he pulled the boyfriend into the station and talked to him. Hal said the young man had been crushed when Courtney suddenly dumped him, but he didn't get any bad vibes from the guy. The kid's only nineteen, and he brought his parents with him, but they sat to the side and let Hal do the interview. The kid seemed very open, and Hal trusted his responses. He said Courtney was hell-bent on getting to this guy in Tennessee that she met online, and when he told her he wouldn't take her there, she dumped him on the spot. Hal said that the guy seemed hurt but not angry."

"So that's a dead end?"

"Hal thinks so."

"How about Capello?" she asked.

"Now there's some good news. Well, good news for Norman and me anyway. You and Sophie are off the hook. Matt had put someone undercover in the campaign two days before he died, and his replacement kept him there."

"Really? They're coming around and beginning to think there's a connection between Capello and the girl's death?"

"Not exactly. The agent is in there for another reason having to do with a case out of Major Crimes, but he's on the lookout for this as well."

"Okay, I guess that's good news."

"For me, it is," Charles said. "I was worried about you being in there."

"I know. You almost had me convinced as well," she responded giving him an appreciative smile. "I'm glad someone is looking at that possibility though."

"He liked the idea of you and Andy stopping in the cafe again and talking to her friends. I'll come along after you get there, but don't let on you know me."

"Of course," she responded. "I'll set that up with Andy. Anything, in particular, we're looking for?"

"No, just get them talking about her and anything they might know about the Tennessee guy. If they say anything relevant, you'll know it."

"Did he find out anything about Waterford's previous convictions?"

"No," Charles responded. "He hasn't had time to look at that, but he did say he's had reports from three of the jurisdictions along the route to Nashville. None were helpful, but at least the local police are looking, and that's a good sign. One gas station attendant remembered them, but he wasn't helpful beyond being able to report that he only remembered there being two people in the car."

"Where was that?"

"Somewhere in Kentucky, I think."

"And they don't have any leads on locating Darius, I assume?" Sarah asked.

"Nothing yet, but he admitted that is their primary focus."

"Poor Bernice. This isn't going to end well."

"Don't give up, sweetie."

* * * * *

"When do you want to go?" Sarah asked Andy the next morning after catching him up on what she had learned from Charles.

"How about this Friday?" Andy responded. "That's the night her friends hang out there."

After they had firmed up their plans, Sarah went into Charles' computer room and found him up to his eyebrows in Singer Featherweight 221 ads. "There are plenty of them out there, hon, but I'm still not comfortable with the online route even if we find one local that we can go see. Let's do it your way and check out quilt shops here and over in Hamilton."

"I agree," she responded, "but you don't want me involved, right?"

Charles hesitated before responding. "Well," he finally said, "I'm beginning to think I need you with me for this investigation. This isn't my kind of detective work."

Sarah laughed and agreed. "Thank goodness," she responded. "I thought you'd never ask."

Chapter 21

"Charlie, it's Hal. Give me a call when you get this. I've got some information that I think you'll like."

Charles and Sarah had just returned from Hamilton where they had looked at two Singer Featherweight 221's. One was old, a 1942 vintage machine which had been reconditioned and was in excellent condition, considering its age. The other was much newer, white, and made in Scotland. The shop owner showed them where the motor was marked "*The Singer Mfg. Co. St. Johns, P.Q., Made in Canada*," and then showed them on the arm where it said "*Made in Great Britain*." He explained that because of the voltage discrepancy between the United States and Europe, the machines produced in Great Britain for the American market were often shipped to Canada for the motor assembly.

"This white machine looks slightly green," Sarah had said as she examined it. The shop owner had explained that there was no record of green machines being produced, and it was generally accepted that this was just a variation in the dye. Sarah loved the quality of the machine but felt she wanted something more traditional. "Let's keep looking," she had whispered to Charles.

"Do you want to drive up to Chicago this weekend and check out those three shops Ruth told us about?" Charles asked as he headed for the telephone which was flashing, signaling that there was a message waiting. "According to Ruth," he continued, "The Sewing Place up there specializes in vintage Singers. We could stay over and have a fancy dinner."

Sarah, seeing the flashing light as well, said, "Go ahead and check our messages and we can talk about it later."

Charles listened to the message and hit the Return Call button. When Detective Halifax answered he said, "Thanks for getting back to me, Charlie."

"Sure," Charles responded and added eagerly, "what have you got?"

"We had a contact from a jurisdiction just over the Tennessee line. A couple of folks at one of the major truck stops remembers someone matching our guy's description causing quite a fracas a couple of weeks before the girl's body was found."

"Was the girl with him?"

"Yep, they were both there," Halifax responded.

"They must see hundreds of people every day. How did they happen to remember him in particular?"

"It's strange, Charlie. Supposedly, the guy was all upset because his car had been stolen. He'd had car trouble—dead battery or something—he'd left the car at the truck stop and walked up to a local service station to get help. When he got back with the mechanic, the car was gone."

"What?" Charles responded, perplexed by what he was hearing. *Who would steal an old broken-down car?*

"What they found strange," the detective continued, "and probably the reason they remembered the incident at all, was that the guy refused to report it to the police."

"That makes sense—a hot car, an arrest warrant, and an underage girl across state lines. I assume the girl was gone too?"

"Yep. They said she'd been in the restaurant earlier, but she was gone too. Supposedly, the guy was hopping mad."

"So, what did he do?"

"He threw a fit, blamed the manager of the truck stop, but left abruptly when they threatened to call the police. He left on foot, and no one knows what happened to him, but the cops down there checked the bus station."

"And?"

"He bought a ticket back to Illinois. He might be right here in town for that matter."

* * * * *

"Sarah, are you up for taking a trip?"

"We're going to Chicago right now?" she asked.

"Nope. We're going in the opposite direction."

"Where?"

"To Tennessee."

"Tennessee?" she exclaimed. "That's hours from here."

"Only about five and we'll stay overnight."

"And why are we doing this?"

"I want to interview the workers at a particular truck stop, and Hal can't get funds released to send a cop down."

He told Sarah what he had learned from Hal, and she listened intently.

"We just might find out what really happened to the girl," Sarah said excitedly. "It sounds like Darius was out of the picture at that point. Do you think she took the car while he was gone?"

"It's possible, I suppose, but apparently the car wasn't running, and she certainly couldn't have fixed it herself."

"I beg your pardon!" Sarah responded with her fists planted on her hips. "And just why would you assume that?" Sarah asked. "If a man can do it, so can a woman," she added defiantly.

"I'll bet you were quite some woman's libber back in the 70s," he responded laughing.

"Never mind that. Just tell me why you think she couldn't fix a car?"

"Well," he began, searching for the right words. "I just can't see when a spoiled young girl named Courtney who got everything she wanted all her life from her indulgent parents would have occasion to learn auto mechanics."

Sarah relaxed and cocked her head thoughtfully. "Perhaps you're right." A few moments later she asked, "Should I tell Bernice?"

"Not yet. Let's go down and see what we can find out. If he's up here, he just might contact her himself."

"I hope so," Sarah responded, but then realized what an awkward position that would put Bernice in.

They left Middletown early the next morning, both filled with enthusiasm. "I think we may be getting to the bottom of this," Charles said. "If we can prove that Darius left the scene at this point, that should clear him or at least leave room for reasonable doubt."

* * * * *

The manager and one waitress were the only people on duty who remembered the incident. Their descriptions exactly matched Hal's report, so Charles didn't think they needed to wait around for the next shift. Neither one could give any information on the girl. The manager hadn't seen her and the waitress only remembered her using the facilities. Charles seemed despondent. "I had hoped for more."

"What did you expect to find out?" Sarah asked.

"I figured there would be more to the story. The local cops didn't have a personal interest in solving this, so I was hoping we'd get a much more detailed story."

"No such luck," Sarah responded. "Shall we look for a place to stay and get some dinner?"

"I guess. Maybe we can stop by here in the morning and talk to the early staff." As he was starting the car, one of the cooks came up to the car wiping his hands on his apron.

"You the folks asking about that car that broke down?"

"Yes," Charles responded. "Did you see what happened?"

"I sure did," but then he added hesitantly, "you a cop?"

"No," he responded which wuss an acceptable version of the truth. *After all, I'm retired and not supposed to be here.*

"Yeah, I saw it. I was out back on a cigarette break. I saw it all."

"Why didn't you tell the police when they were asking about it?"

"Well, it wasn't no regular cigarette, if you know what I mean. I didn't want to get into any trouble, so I just laid low while they was here, but I saw it all."

"Would you tell us now?" Sarah asked with a friendly smile. "We sure don't care what you were smoking, but we'd like to find out what happened to our friends."

"Well, see the guy tried to get that heap of junk started up, but he couldn't. He swore a good bit, excuse me ma'am, and then he left the girl in the car and walked up the block, I guess to get help."

"What happened next?" Charles asked, attempting to modulate his tone so it didn't sound like an interrogation, something his wife often accused him of.

"Okay," the man continued. "So, in the meantime, Old Artie came along. He seemed really interested in the girl. Asked all about where she was going and where she came from. Then he had his head under the hood for a while. He looked real happy to help out, and before you know it, he had that car running." Charles wanted to ask who Old Artie was, but didn't want to sidetrack the cook's account of what happened.

"So what happened then?" he said instead.

"Old Artie hopped right in that car, and they took off. She was laughing, so I figured they were going to go catch up with the guy she came with, but that ain't what happened."

"It isn't?" Sarah asked encouraging him to go on.

"No. When the guy got back here with help and saw that his car and his girl were gone, he kicked the gas pump— thought he was going to knock it over. What a temper that guy had. And the language, excuse me ma'am, was something you wouldn't want to hear."

Hoping the man would continue, Charles said, "This Artie, an old guy, huh?" Charles asked.

"No. Artie's no older than me. I don't know why they call him Old Artie. They just do. I know he was homeless for a while, but he's been living across the street in that rooming house for the past year or so."

"Is he there now?"

"To tell you the truth, I don't think I've seen that man since he fixed that car and drove off. Never saw any of them again."

Charles and Sarah thanked the man profusely. Charles pulled a couple of twenties out of his wallet, and the man accepted them saying, "Oh, you don't need to pay me," as he quickly slipped the bills into his apron pocket.

Sarah and Charles drove directly across the street and rang the manager's doorbell.

* * * * *

"I have no idea what became of that scumbag," Mrs. Roberts was saying. "He lived here for about a year and never paid on time. I'd have to toss his stuff out on the curb before he'd pay. I finally figured out what day he got his government check and that's the day I'd put his stuff out," she said with a cackle, "and he'd sign the check over to me to get back in."

"Clever trick," Sarah said, hoping to keep the woman talking.

"It didn't cover the rent, but I let it slide. There something wrong with the guy. Why are you two looking for him anyway? You seem like nice folks. He's not family, is he?"

Sarah looked at Charles, and he shrugged a look that she figured meant that they had nothing to lose. They told the woman the whole story, and she listened intently.

"You mean that girl that was killed down in Nashville a couple of months ago? I thought that looked like the same girl that was walking around outside the truck stop over there."

"You saw her?" Sarah said with surprise.

"And you recognized her?" Charles added, suddenly sitting up straighter in his chair and giving her his full attention.

"Sure. Her picture was in the paper every day back then. She'd been missing, and there was a big reward. I think she was the daughter of some big politician up north and he was trying to find her."

"Did Artie know about her?"

"Sure. I called him down to look out the window at her. I told him I thought it was the same girl. He grabbed the paper and stared at it. She had this beautiful long red hair just like the girl in the picture. I told Artie we should call the police and try to get the reward."

"What did he say?"

"He didn't say anything. He just went into the kitchen, and I think he went out the back door."

"Did you call the police?"

"No," she said defensively, "and I got my reasons. I didn't want the cops snooping around here. Matter of fact," she added thoughtfully, "I think that's the last time I ever saw Old Artie."

"Do you have any idea where he might be now?" Charles asked.

"No idea. I've got his stuff in the back. All he had was some clothes and a box of letters from his brother down in Florida. Do you want to see them?"

Sarah and Charles didn't stay overnight in Tennessee. Charles put a call in to Detective Halifax and got the ball rolling.

Chapter 22

A secluded area along Florida's Gulf coast …
    The man pulled the car over and parked it by the side of the road. The tank registered empty, and the steam from the engine had been nearly blinding. "Bad luck," he muttered to himself as he started walking toward the Gulf and his brother's trailer. "Nothing but bad luck my whole life. Can't ever catch a break."

Artie thought his luck had finally changed in Tennessee when he looked across the street at that pretty young girl and immediately recognized her. The police had been to the restaurant passing out fliers. He had studied the picture back then imagining what it would be like to find her. He pictured himself enjoying the fortune the wealthy father would pay to get his daughter back.

He knew he had to play it cool. He offered to help her get the car started and told her they'd go find her boyfriend. It was working, too, until she realized what he was doing.

Why did she have to fight him? He sure couldn't collect with nothing but a body to return. "I didn't mean to kill her," he said aloud but didn't even believe it himself. It hadn't been the first time he'd felt that pull … that desire from deep inside to squeeze the life out of a living thing … but he'd never given in to it before, at least not with a person. He wondered if he'd get another chance.

Artie's life had been a succession of tragedies, or bad luck, as he sometimes called them. His father's mysterious death, the loss of his childhood home, being expelled from school, his inability to hold down a job. His brother had gotten away from it all and Artie thought he should have done the same. He wished he'd stuck closer to his brother. His brother always got the breaks.

"Well, I'm down here now, and things are going to start looking up." Once the car broke down in Tennessee, he left it and hitched rides with truckers across Georgia, glad to put miles between him and the girl's body.

He was able to hotwire an old car parked behind a gas station once he got to Florida. He'd figured it was waiting for repairs. He'd had to stop along the way to work on it just to keep it going. When it stopped only a few miles from his destination, he just left it and continued on foot.

He'd been traveling for a month or so he figured. He'd taken a few odd jobs just to keep a few dollars in his pocket. He's used a trucker's cell phone to change the address on his government check so he'd have money when he got to his brother's place.

It was growing dark as he crossed the expanse of thorny scrub grass and sand. He could smell the Gulf just beyond the next bend. It was a deserted area which pleased him. He'd had enough of people for a long while.

He looked at the crumpled map which he'd studied for years, planning to improve his lot in life by following in his brother's footsteps. "It's just a little farther up the road," he told himself with a guttural sound of pleasure. He turned onto the rutted lane that led past the dilapidated trailer half hidden by weeds and discarded trash.

"Guess who?" he hollered as he opened the rusty door and stepped into the abandoned trailer.

The distant sirens were growing closer and, as he turned to look out into the dusk, the flashing lights of a dozen police cars were fast approaching the trailer.

"Can't ever catch a break."

Chapter 23

"How did they know that this Artie guy was in Florida?" Sophie asked.

The Undercover Sleuths were all sitting around the dining room table at the Parker's house celebrating the capture of the real killer and the fact that Darius was now off the hook for murder. Sarah had just served a pancake breakfast along with turkey sausage and a bowl of thinly sliced strawberries for those who wanted to add them to their stacks.

"Well," Charles responded as he reached for the can of fat-free whipped cream, which he squirted generously on top of his strawberry-covered pancakes, "first of all, we guessed."

"What do you mean?"

"Sarah and I read the letters from the brother that were in the rooming house where this Artie guy had been staying."

"And he was encouraging Artie to come down to Florida?" Andy asked.

"Quite the opposite. In every letter, the brother told him not to come. He clearly had no interest in reconnecting with Artie, but we found several maps of Florida with the brother's area circled and a couple of notes that laid out several routes to the Gulf side of Florida. It just seemed logical that the guy would be heading that way, although the last letter from the brother was dated two years ago. We knew he might not even be there anymore, and, as it turned out, he wasn't."

"But we called Detective Halifax and told him there was a chance they might find Old Artie there," Sarah added.

"As it turned out," Charles continued, "Hal had an even better idea. There were several government check stubs in the shoebox, and Hal checked, on the off chance that the guy had been stupid enough to submit a change of address."

"Surely he wasn't," Sophie commented.

"Yes, he was just that stupid," Charles responded. "He called ahead and had his checks mailed to his brother's address … at least what he thought was his brother's address."

"And that's where they found him?"

"It sure was. According to Hal, our guy was standing in the doorway of his brother's abandoned trailer, just waiting for the police cars to reach him."

"Did he put up a fight?" Norman asked.

"He just mumbled something about never catching a break, but he went willingly. Hal said the local cops down there are arranging extradition to Nashville where he'll stand trial for the girl's murder."

"Any chance he'll get off?" Sophie asked.

"None," Charles responded. "Not only did he have her jewelry in his possession, but those previously unidentified fingerprints were his."

"So I guess our work is done," Sophie announced proudly with a glob of whipped cream dripping down her chin.

"Not exactly," Sarah said. "We still don't know what happened to Darius."

"That's not entirely true," Bernice said, looking guilty as she lowered her eyes and laid her fork down.

"Bernice?" Sarah said. "What do you mean?"

Bernice was quiet for a few moments and then spoke in a soft voice. The group had to lean in to hear her. "He called me a couple of weeks ago and told me he is right here in Middletown."

"And you didn't tell us?" Sarah said in a stunned tone. "Bernice, what were you thinking?"

"I'm sorry. He told me he was here and that he was hiding out until the police found the real killer. He knew that if they picked him up, he would be charged with the girl's murder. He told me he didn't do it and I believed him. I'm sorry, Sarah and everyone else, but I had to keep it to myself just hoping the killer would be caught."

Andy was sitting next to Bernice quietly, but, like everyone else, had stopped eating. He put his arm around her shoulder and gently patted her. "They understand," he murmured.

"You knew this?" Charles said to Andy, and his friend nodded his head almost imperceptibly.

"I knew, and I believed him too," Andy responded. "I spoke with him, and he admitted that he deserved to be charged with the crimes he had committed, but he was also sure if they found him, he'd go down for Courtney's death, and he was probably right."

"I suppose that's true," Charles replied, still looking upset about it. "But …"

"He insisted that he had nothing to do with it," Andy continued, "and he told the same story you told about going for help with the car and returning to find the car and the girl both gone. He had no idea what had happened to them. That's when he decided to just come back to Middletown."

"Did he have anything else to say?" Charles asked.

"He said that he planned to turn himself in just as soon as the real killer was caught. I think he meant it, Charles. I really do."

"Do you know where he is?" Charles asked. He was immediately sorry that he had asked the question because if Andy told him, he'd be bound by professional ethics to report it to Hal. As it was, he'd have to tell him that the guy was in town.

"I didn't ask and he didn't say. Bernice and I talked about it, and we decided to trust him. He didn't have to call Bernice, you know. He wasn't asking for anything except her trust and to let her know he was okay."

Everyone except Bernice went back to their meal eventually, but without the gusto they previously had. Later as Sarah was taking the dishes off the table and Sophie was refilling the coffee cups, Charles cell phone rang.

He glanced at the display and saw that it was Halifax. "I need to take this," he said as he stood and moved out of the dining room. *How much should I tell him?* he wondered.

He returned a few minutes later with a broad grin.

"Darius Mitchell just turned himself in."

Everyone except Bernice cheered. She laid her head on Andy's shoulder and wept, but everyone knew they were tears of relief.

Charles smiled across the table at his wife's new friend and said, "You were right, Bernice." She smiled back at him through her tears.

* * * * *

Sarah and Bernice had cleared the table and refreshed everyone's coffee when Charles asked that everyone remain around the table for a few minutes longer. "Hal had some other news too," he said. Turning toward Bernice, he added, "For you, Bernice."

She looked at him with curiosity and a touch of dread. "What?" She asked cautiously.

"There were other arrests made today."

"And that affects me?" she responded clearly confused.

"It sure does. Hal told me about this a few days ago, but he asked that I not talk about it until the arrests were made. It seems that a major credit card trafficking ring out of Central America was infiltrated by the FBI and our police came in contact with them while trying to link Darius to your credit card fiasco. It turns out these guys have been placing skimmers in ATMs and gas pumps all over the Midwest, and that's how your credit cards were compromised," Charles announced excitedly, pleased to be able to present her with this good news.

"I don't understand," Bernice responded without much expression.

Not exactly the reaction I expected. Charles realized his own enthusiasm had interfered with his ability to explain what had happened clearly. "Okay," he said. "Let me explain about these skimmers." At this point, the entire group was giving him their complete attention.

"First of all, is everyone here aware of your credit card problem, Bernice?"

"Yes, I told Andy, and the rest of you were involved from the beginning," she responded.

"Okay, so what we're talking about is a small device that criminals attach to card readers on ATMs, gas pumps, or any kind of payment terminal where you might be inserting your credit card. These are called skimmers, and they are able to capture your credit card information once you insert your card."

Bernice was astonished. "Are you saying it wasn't Darius that stole my credit card information?"

"That's what I'm saying."

"And this is how my credit cards numbers ended up down to Central America?"

"Yep. That's what Hal told me."

"I can hardly believe this," Bernice said, sitting back in her chair and looking stunned. "It wasn't Darius?" she repeated rhetorically.

"I've heard about the skimmers," Norman commented, "but I had no idea they'd made their way to Middletown. I use my credit or debit card for almost everything," he added. "I assume the skimmers read debit cards as well?"

"Yes, but to get the most out of a debit card, they would need your pin number. Some of the skimmers have small cameras built in to read your actions as you punch in the numbers so it's always good to shield the pad when you're inputting your number."

"This is really scary," Sophie exclaimed. "I don't think I'll ever use a credit card again. But," she added, "That would be very inconvenient, especially at gas pumps."

"Despite skimmers, credit cards are still probably safer than shopping with cash," Andy interjected.

"I agree," Charles said. "If you're interested, Hal gave me some pointers on how to avoid skimmers."

"I sure want to know," Sarah responded. "Wait while I make another pot of coffee, and why don't we move to the living room where it's more comfortable."

Sophie followed Sarah into the kitchen and reached into the tote bag she had placed on the kitchen table earlier.

"What's that?" Sarah asked.

"Well, I didn't know if you'd need sticky buns with your breakfast, but when I saw you were having pancakes, I knew you wouldn't want me to put them out, but now that we're going to probably be here for a while, perhaps …?"

Sarah burst out laughing, "Of course, you may serve your sticky buns. Everyone will be delighted. Just grab a handful of napkins and six dessert plates. There's a platter on the second shelf you can use to serve them."

"I'm so pleased for Bernice," Sophie said as she arranged the buns on the platter. "I don't know what the courts will decide about Darius, but she realizes that he has to pay for the crimes he committed, and that doesn't bother her. She must be very relieved to know he won't be falsely accused of murder."

"And relieved that he didn't steal her credit card numbers. Now I'm wondering if he actually took the money from her checking account."

"He did," Bernice said stepping into the kitchen at that moment. "I just asked Charles that question, and he said it would require a debit card and pin number to wipe out my bank account. I never got a debit card."

"So it was Darius that took the money out of your account?"

"Yes, when he called me he admitted it and said he was going to pay me back every penny. Of course, I've heard that before, and I've blindly believed him, but I think there's a possibility he just might do it this time."

As soon as the group had reassembled in the living room and were relaxing in front of the fire, Charles shared some of the information he had on avoiding skimmers.

"First of all," he began, "Hal said to check out the ATM or gas pump for any signs of tampering, like scratches or imperfections that probably shouldn't be there. Then notice if there is anything around the area where you insert the card, anything a different color or that looks or feels like it might have been added to the original machine. Take a look at other gas pumps or nearby card readers and make sure they look like the one you're using. Then there's location to consider."

"Location?" Sophie repeated. "What do you mean?"

"Criminals need time to install the skimmer, and they'll pick ones in the more secluded spots. Those are the ones to avoid. Banks tend to have cameras, so those are ones they are likely to be safer to use. Hal suggests avoiding ones on the street."

"I have a chip on my card. Is that safer?" Norman asked.

"Hal said your information can't be compromised when you're using a card with a chip, so use that whenever possible."

"I'm still worried about using my card," Sophie grumbled.

"Don't be, Sophie," Charles responded. "If you get skimmed, just notify your credit card company right away. They won't hold you responsible for the charges made by these crooks. Just keep your eye on your charges and make sure they're all yours. Hal also said that you should trust your instincts. If something just seems wrong, put your card away and leave."

The remainder of the morning was spent in relaxed conversation among the newly formed group of friends. At one point Sarah announced that she had a surprise, and she left the room, returning in a few moments with a familiar black box—familiar at least to most of the group.

Andy asked, "What's everyone smiling about? Am I missing something?"

Sarah opened the box and pulled out her shiny new Singer Featherweight 221. "Birthdate 1943," Sarah announced proudly.

"Might that be your birthdate as well?" Sophie asked deviously.

"It might be, and then it might not be," Sarah responded with a coy grin.

"Either way," Charles announced, "you're all invited Saturday night to celebrate."

Chapter 24

The Undercover Sleuths were sitting together in the courtroom forming a support group which filled the row directly behind Darius and his defense attorney. The attorney had been successful in getting Bernice's stolen car charges dropped, and any connection to Courtney Waterford's murder had become moot. That left Darius with the two original charges: Grand Theft Auto and Failure to Appear.

Darius stood next to his attorney with his head held high when the judge requested his plea. "My client is pleading guilty on all counts," the lawyer announced.

"Is this true?" the judge asked Darius directly.

"Yes, sir," he responded respectfully.

"We are requesting a reduced sentence," the lawyer added, "due in part to the fact that my client turned himself in voluntarily."

"What took him so long?" the judge asked with a frown.

"There was a manhunt in process and much circumstantial evidence pointing toward my client for the murder of the daughter of a prominent politician." Everyone in the courtroom knew who he was referring to, but he didn't mention the Waterford case.

"My client," he continued, "knew he was innocent but feared prosecution. He hid out until the murderer was caught."

"Your client doesn't have much faith in the legal system," the judge responded, still frowning. "What are you asking for?" he finally asked.

"We're requesting a reduced sentence of two to five years and that he be placed in the Evanston Minimum Security facility where he would have the opportunity to participate in the computer applications program run by Andrew Burgess, who happens to be in the courtroom at this time. Mr. Burgess has agreed to this plan."

"I've heard of Mr. Burgess' program," the judge responded, glancing around the room. Andy gave a slight nod which the judge acknowledged with his own. Andy had been volunteering at the prison since his own incarceration some time ago and had sent many inmates out into the world with a new and viable skill.

The judge turned to the prosecutor and raised an eyebrow, nonverbally asking for his response.

The young prosecutor was eager to get this case resolved and out of the newspapers. The political and community pressure to solve the girl's murder had been devastating. *All that time spent chasing down the wrong man*, he admonished himself. The entire fiasco had not been good for his career and most likely had negated any opportunity for advancement. He was eager to have the whole thing behind him.

"No objections, Your Honor."

The judge turned to Darius Mitchell giving him a stern look. "Are you willing to enroll and participate in the program, young man?" he asked.

"Yes, Your Honor," Darius responded, still standing tall and proud. The judge agreed to the recommendation of the defense attorney since there was no objection from the prosecution. He sentenced Darius to two to five years at Evanston with the requirement that he participate in the computer applications program.

As the six friends were preparing to leave the courtroom, Bernice approached the attorney and asked to speak with Darius for a moment. They glanced up at the judge who nodded his approval. She reached up to hug the boy she had cared for and who had grown into a man. She wished him well and told him she'd be praying for his success.

"I'm going to do it, Mama. I'm going to do it for you." It was the first time he'd called her Mama, and she fought tears. But by the time she walked toward her new friends who were waiting at the back of the courtroom, she was smiling joyfully.

"Let's all meet at La Bonita's for a celebration. I'm in the mood for nachos and quesadillas," Andy announced.

"They also serve rattlesnake fillets," Sophie teased, "and cactus fries."

"I'll settle for a couple of bean burritos," Charles declared, looking at his wife proudly. "See, I'm learning how to eat heart-healthy."

"You sure are," she said squeezing his arm as he walked her to the car. "It's finally over, Charles. I think we should officially disband the Undercover Sleuths and swear off detecting for life. What do you think?"

"I agree, but I don't think that will ever happen."

LEFT HOLDING THE BAG

See full quilt on back cover.

Bernice's collection of vintage feed sacks inspired Sophie to make this 62″ × 84½″ four-patch quilt. Whether made from feed sacks or 1930s reproduction fabrics, your quilt will have a lovely nostalgic feel.

MATERIALS

Blocks: Assorted fabrics (half light, half dark) to total 3⅜ yards

Cornerstones: Assorted fabrics to total ⅝ yard

Sashing and border: 2¼ yards

Binding: ⅝ yard

Backing: 5⅛ yards

Batting: 70″ × 92″

Project Instructions

Seam allowances are ¼". WOF = width of fabric.

MAKE THE BLOCKS

1. Cut a total of 32 strips 3½" × WOF.

2. Sew together 2 contrasting strips. Press toward the dark.

3. Cut the strip set into 3½" sections.

4. Sew together 2 sections, matching the contrasting fabrics. Press. Make 88.

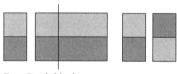

Four-Patch blocks

CUT THE SASHING, BORDER, CORNERSTONES, AND BORDER CORNERS

1. From the sashing/border fabric, cut 11 strips 6½" × WOF. Subcut 157 rectangles 6½" × 2" for the sashing and 38 rectangles 6½" × 2¼" for the border.

2. From the cornerstone fabric, cut 4 strips 2" × WOF. Subcut 70 squares 2" × 2" for the sashing cornerstones.

3. From cornerstone fabric, cut 3 strips 2¼" × WOF. Subcut 4 squares 2¼" × 2¼" for the border corners and 34 rectangles 2¼" × 2" for the border cornerstones.

ASSEMBLE THE INNER QUILT

1. Starting with a block, alternate 8 blocks and 7 sashing rectangles; sew together into a row. Press toward the blocks. Make 11 rows.

2. Starting with a rectangle, alternate 8 sashing rectangles and 7 sashing cornerstones; sew together into a sashing strip. Press toward the cornerstones. Make 10 sashing strips.

3. Starting with a row of blocks, alternate the 11 rows and the 10 sashing strips; sew together. Press toward the rows of blocks.

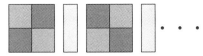

Alternate blocks with sashing.

Alternate sashing with cornerstones.

PROJECT

ADD THE BORDER AND FINISH THE QUILT

1. Starting with a rectangle, alternate 11 border rectangles and 10 border cornerstones; sew together. Press toward the cornerstones. Make 2. Sew to the sides of the quilt. Press.

2. Starting with a rectangle, alternate 8 border rectangles and 7 border cornerstones 2″ × 2¼″; sew together. Add a border corner (2¼″ square) to each end. Press toward the cornerstones and corners. Make 2. Sew to the top and bottom of the quilt. Press.

3. Layer the pieced top with batting and backing. Quilt and bind as desired.

A Note
from the Author

I want to thank my many loyal readers for the hours you have spent reading this series. You have stayed with me for the long haul, following Sarah and her cohorts from the beginning.

I hope these stories have inspired you to find ways to make your own retirement years fulfilling and fun. And if you aren't already a quilter, I hope you'll give it (or some other creative outlet) a try.

I love hearing from you and hope you will continue to contact me on my blog or send me an email.

Best wishes,

Carol Dean Jones
caroldeanjones.com
quiltingcozy@gmail.com

READER'S GUIDE:
A QUILTING COZY SERIES
by Carol Dean Jones

1. Why do you think Bernice was so reluctant to see what her foster son was doing to her?

2. Our elderly family members need to tell their stories, but we are often reluctant to listen. Why do you think this is? Is today's generation interested in bygone days?

3. Several times in this series, Sarah mentions that the gentle hum of her sewing machine helps to calm her in times of stress. What other things have you noticed that Sarah does to maintain balance in her life?

4. Charles said that life is meant to be lived with gusto right up to the end. Discuss how the various characters in this series have done just that.

5. Prior to Matt's death, the Police Department was not willing to look at suspects other than Darius. However, after Matt's death, Detective Halifax began working with Charles to find the real killer. What do you think motivated him to change his focus?

6. If you were making a movie of this series, whom would you cast?